# WILLEM

## LEON MICHAELS

# Books by Leon Michaels

The Path Home

From the Mists of Darkness

Task Force Nemesis

Tales From The Bench*

The Hanover Throne

The Echelon Factor

The Morbius Expedition

The Bellus Project

Three Against The Darkness

Random Acts Of Science Fiction


"The Crane Equation Trilogy"

The Crane Equation: The Early Years

The Crane Equation: Rebuilding a Nation

The Crane Equation: The Crane Legacy


"The Black Ops Series"

Operation Damocles

Operation Dokkaebi

Operation Yofune-Nushi

Operation Kartikeya

The Black Orchid


"The Twenty-First Special Operations Group"

Book One: Family

Book Two: Operators


*Contributor & Editor

# Acknowledgements

To my bride who read and commented on the draft of this story, telling me it was good, but needed a bit more.

So I added about 1500 more words and it still needs more according to her.

I really need to look up the definition of 'more' because this is all I have with this story.

# A Time of Passing

As he placed the last stone on the grave, Willem pondered his situation, since the old man beneath the rocks had been his life as long as he could remember. Before his death, the old man told Willem that he was twenty annuals old, and that his destiny was beyond the mountains to the west. He stood, wiped his hands on his buckskins, then set the marker on the grave. It was only because of the old man, that he knew the date of his death. Willem had cut February 19, 2261 into the steel plate he had made for his grave marker. Willem had to laugh at the marker since he never knew the old man's name, or even how old he was. He was always just old man to him.

Willem walked away from the grave thinking how peacefully the old man had died. He had laid down for the evening and sometime during the night had died in his sleep. Willem had tried to waken him, so they could break fast this morn, and was pleased the old man had died so peacefully. As hard as the labors the old man required from him each day, he was always concerned about his health and growth. Willem always ate well despite the hard times they often endured, and the old man worked him hard to build his muscle and endurance for whatever the old man had planned for him.

The old man taught him to read and write in an old language from the fragile books he kept in a box he called the fridge. Now he had to decide what to take with him since he knew he had to complete the journey the old man said he had to one day take to find his destiny. Willem knew he would take the old book of maps the old man taught him to read, along with the book of words that was properly named a Dictionary. But whatever he could not carry, he knew the people who inhabited these woods would take whatever he left for their own purposes.

Willem went to the forge and selected the tools he might need to work the bits and pieces of steel he could find later into tools. He had made his own knives and lance tip. The arrowheads for his longbow were crafted under the guidance of the old man to be properly balanced, so the arrow would fly true. His blades were balanced for throwing if necessary, and sharp to do the work they may be called to do.

He spent the rest of the day constructing a travois to carry the tools and extra clothing he might need for this trip. His pack would hold the things he would have immediate need of along with his short rations as his smoked meats and grains would be carried on the travois. Willem checked each of the two dozen long arrow shafts for straightness as he filled his quiver. He had the makings of another dozen on the travois along with two bows he was still working on.

Willem checked, then rechecked every item he was taking and insured the books he was taking were carefully wrapped in oil skins to keep them from getting wet. He was only taking six books plus the book of maps that the old man always referred to as the Rand-McNally. Years before the old man had marked one of the maps with where they were living. Willem had grown to be a man in what the map had marked as the Mark Twain National Forest just northwest of a place marked as West Plains in an area once known as Missouri.

He remembered once going to West Plains when he was much younger with the old man to do some trading with the handful of people who lived there. Willem once asked the old man what had happened to the towns and cities on the map that they had visited. The old man said there had been a global war followed by disease and famine which nearly wiped out humanity. He only told Willem that it had occurred long before even he was born, and humanity was still suffering from it all.

Willem checked the travois one last time to insure it was securely tied together with rawhide and that the curved, steel runners were secure to insure the travois slid across the ground with as little drag as possible. He had two water bladders on the travois already filled from the well and a smaller one to carry to drink from as he walked. One last check of his pack and he was ready to leave the only home he had ever known.

He double checked to insure he had the small, metal box in the bottom of his pack. The old man said it contained his destiny, but it could only be opened over the mountains. Willem had handled the box many times but could not find a way to open it.

But the old man said that if anything ever happened to him to take it with him and go west over the mountains.

Willem took a deep breath, picked up the limbs to the travois and began his trek west.

# Step by Step

It was written long ago that the longest journey begins with a single step. Willem had been walking for nearly three weeks and had yet to leave the old state of Missouri. He had decided from the start to avoid the roads and main trails west in order not to attract attention. This slowed him down especially when crossing creeks and rivers, but he did help him avoid travelers that may have hindered his journey.

Willem did walk just deep enough into the brush away from the main trails heading west to avoid detection, but he could see them and used them as a guide. As he skirted each town, if he could he located the name of the town, then marked it on his map with the date of travel as a record of his journey. Each day was marked with a simple tick mark at the top of the map each evening before darkness fell upon him.

He often thought it would be nice to have a horse to help with his load but had to smile at the memory of Old Blue, the horse he was raised with. But it was not only the memory of the horse that made him smile, but what had happened to Old Blue when he turned sixteen annuals.

Several months before he turned sixteen, the old man gave him a job to deal with. Willem was to build his own cabin on the other side of the forge away from the cabin he had been raised in. The old man had made it clear to him that the bed was to be large enough for two people. Willem first laid it out on paper, then on the ground, adjusting his design as he developed a visual concept of it.

Years before Willem's first memory, the old man had developed a method of moving water from the creek at the bottom of the ridge they lived on up to the cabin. There was a water wheel which powered what the old man called an Archimedes Screw which moved the water up into a tank made of wood which was about a meter taller than the roof of the cabin.

Willem had helped the old man repair the wheel and screw several times over the years and understood the principle. When the water level fell to a point in the reservoir tank, they would engage the wheel which powered the screw and lifted the water up to the tank. From the tank, water was piped into the cabin by wooden pipes glued together by a glue made from tree sap. Even the valve inside the house was carved from wood.

It had taken nearly six months for Willem to build his own cabin and plumb it. Inside he had a fireplace to cook, along with a sink to wash his meager cookware in. He had also constructed a small tub to bath in with a hole in the bottom to drain it back down the ridge. The old man inspected his work daily and would only comment if he felt Willem had made an error which he gave Willem a chance to explain his reasoning.

Once the cabin was ready to live in, the old man rode off on Old Blue telling Willem he would be back in a few days and to make sure the chores were done while he was gone. When the old man returned he had a woman with him. She was shorter than the old man and slender. Her hair was dark, and not yet showing grey in it, but Willem could tell she was much older than he was.

She introduced herself to Willem as Margaret and moved into his cabin. That night she introduced Willem to his manhood and taught him how to make love to a woman. She cooked, cleaned the cabin and helped in the garden during the day, while giving herself to him whenever he desired her. The old man never interacted with Margaret during her stay with Willem, except for the minor things that were common around the cabin and forge.

A month after she arrived, Margaret left riding Old Blue after a night of intense passion. After she left the old man asked Willem how he enjoyed the woman. They talked for a short time before the old man told Willem he had only bargained with her for two weeks. The additional two weeks she stayed was because she wanted to stay and enjoy Willem's bed. Willem never learned where Margaret came from or left for, and never saw her again. But twice during trips to a small town with the old man, he found the time, and a female to enjoy for an hour or two before they returned to the cabin.

He spent the night just west of Washburn Missouri after searching the ruins of the town for anything useful to his trip. His

11

only real gain from the search was two chickens and an old piece of canvas that was still intact and was more than large enough to cover himself or use as a ground cloth. It was just after mid-day when he found himself making a decision he had hoped to avoid.

On the old road, a wagon passed him being pulled by a single horse. He had stood next to a tree to hide his presence from anyone who might look in his direction and watched as a family rode past. To him it looked as if everything they owned was in the wagon along with a young girl riding on the back. A few minutes after they passed he heard what he thought was a gunshot then he could hear the screams of the woman. He squatted and released his hold on the travois then dropped his pack. Quickly he moved towards the screaming as the sounds increased to include the girl's voice as she was screaming no. He had his long bow at the ready with an arrow already notched when he finally was in position to see what was happening.

The man who had been driving the wagon was slumped over the side of the wagon, but the woman and the girl were on the ground being raped. Willem quickly scanned to insure he had the count correct of the men involved and counted five men along with five saddled horses. He pulled four additional arrows from his quiver and moved to a better spot to shoot from. Two of the men were actively raping the females with one man holding the arms of the woman while the other two men were pilfering through the wagon for valuables.

Willem stuck the extra arrows into the ground as he stood to fire. His first arrow was directed towards the man standing in the wagon and even as it was in flight Willem was reaching for the next arrow which he sent into the man standing by the wagon watching the rape, waiting his turn. His third arrow went into the man holding the woman's arms. The men who were raping the females were so caught up in what they were doing they died in the act not realizing their friends had already been killed.

The old man had made Willem practice with a bow for hours when he was young to hunt for food. Willem's aim was true with each arrow finding the heart of each man even from the side. Willem stood nearly two meters tall and was a big, strong man. Many men could not pull the long bow back due to the strength of the wood, but Willem had trained with it and had carved it himself finding the spot where it produced enough power to send an arrow farther than a regular bow and with accuracy.

The woman was able to get out from under the man on top of her and was trying to remove the man on the young girl when Willem stepped out of the tree line. Willem's buckskins were streaked with the staining juices of blackberries and other plants to give it the effect of blending in with the flora of the forest. His blond hair was covered with a piece of coarse woven cloth he had obtained through trading a few years before while his skin was deeply tanned from working in the sun for hours each day.

Willem moved to the young female and jerked the dead rapist off her before moving from man to man to insure they were dead. Once he was sure they were safe, he cut the arrowheads from each shaft to save them for future use and dropped them into his small bag around his waist. Willem slung the bow over his back then gently lowered the dead husband to the ground. The woman was holding the young female as the girl was crying and shaking from the experience.

"Who are you?" The woman asked.

"My name is Willem. Are you badly hurt?"

"No, I'll survive but Martha is only twelve."

"Listen, try to take her off the road into the woods while I tend to these outlaws."

The woman nodded then stood lifting the girl up. Both females clothing was badly torn, but the mother helped the girl back into the woods and just sat down and watched Willem. He picked up everything the men had tossed out of the wagon back into it and led the horse off the road back into the woods. Willem noticed the water jug under the wagon seat and took it to the woman before going back onto the road.

Willem moved the husband's body off the road then took stock of what was left. He gathered the horses and tied them up inside the tree line before dealing with the men. Willem found two muzzle loading rifles where the females were being raped and set them aside. He knew about them but had never fired one. He completely stripped each man before dragging the bodies into the woods on the other side of the road. Once everything was clear of the road he took a piece of scrub brush and swept the road to hide the blood of his kills the best he could.

He checked on the females before looking in the wagon for a shovel. He was lucky in that there was one on board and began to dig a grave for the husband. Soon the woman came to help as the girl had gone to sleep. As Willem took a blanket from one of the horses, the woman took everything valuable from her husband's body as she quietly cried at her loss. Willem carefully wrapped the body in the blanket then lowered it into the shallow grave. Once the dirt was back in the hole, Willem began gathering rocks to cover it and to hinder animals from digging up the body for food. Once the woman saw what he was doing she helped him gather rocks.

Willem checked the sun's position and knew he would not make much more distance before he had to stop before dark and he now had two females needing help.

"Lady, what is your name?"

"Susan, my name is Susan."

"Susan, it will be dark before long, and we need to move away from here and find a place to camp before dark."

"Alright. Willem, thank you."

"You're welcome, now wake up the girl and let's get her on the wagon. I need to go get my things and then we'll move further back into the woods for the night."

Willem gathered up his travois and pack then returned to place all the clothing and things taken off the outlaw's bodies on the travois. He tied the horses to the back of the wagon before having the woman just lead the horse pulling the wagon as he walked in front to insure the way was as smooth as possible. He walked until he found a small stream and told Susan this was where they would make camp.

The girl was still in shock from what had happened to her and Willem just erected a small shelter for her and her mother from a piece of canvas from the wagon. Susan cleared out a place for a fire then found rocks to make a fire circle. Willem cautioned her to make a small fire as she gathered dead wood. She made a meal from smoked meats from the wagon and they ate in silence as the girl slept. Willem rigged his own shelter then went to the creek to bath.

He heard the woman behind him as he sat in the creek cleaning the dirt and sweat of the day off his body. A couple minutes later Susan came and sat down beside him and washed herself.

"Willem, George was a drunk and an abusive husband, but he did take care of Martha and me. Thank you again for saving Martha and me from God only knows what once they were done with us in that road."

Nothing more was said as Willem finished cleaning himself and then moving away from the creek leaving Susan to finish washing herself. In the waning light of day Willem went through the clothing then the saddlebags on the horses for valuables. He put everything on a saddle blanket next to the female's shelter before laying out his ground cloth and stripped down for the night. Susan checked on Martha when she returned to camp then walked over to Willem's shelter and let her dress fall off onto the ground. She pulled his blanket off him and laid down beside him.

"Willem, I stopped loving George a long time ago because of his drinking and beating me. But I couldn't leave him because of Martha. Use me tonight if you want because it is all I have to give you for saving us today."

Willem was confused by this woman since she had been raped earlier and he had seen tears when they buried her husband.

"No Susan, you owe me nothing. Besides, I now have two horses to help me in my journey. Go, be with your daughter."

Susan leaned over and kissed him on his cheek before getting up and moving back to the pad Martha was lying on. Willem just lay quietly listening to the night and Martha's nightmares as the night consumed him pondering how little he knew about life away from the old man's forge.

Martha had slept fitfully during the night and was still asleep until Susan woke her to eat something once the cooking was done. The girl just huddled off to the side with her knees drawn up to her chin and her arms wrapped around them. They broke camp and Susan moved to Martha and talked to her quietly for several minutes before Martha got up and climbed up on the wagon.

During breakfast Susan and Willem had talked about the female's future. Susan told Willem that George was taking them to Coffeyville Kansas because he heard there was work there. They were going to return to Cassville where she had kin and try to survive, maybe find another man who would take care of them.

Willem kept two of the outlaw's horses and two saddles. He tossed the extra saddles into the back of the wagon and tied the extra horses to the back of the wagon. Willem left everything at the camp and guided the wagon and females back to the road away from George's grave. Nothing was said as Susan took the reins and moved back down the road away from Willem. He watched as they disappeared down the road before moving back to the campsite and starting his own journey west.

Susan had given Willem some of the salt pork they had on the wagon along with a few other items of food. He rigged the travois to the saddle of one horse and adjusted the saddle of the one he was going to ride.  If Susan made it back to Cassville with the other horses and saddles, she should be able to get a good price for them to give her a decent stake in taking care of Martha.

Of the gear he took off the outlaws, only one knife met his standards for quality which he kept and gave the rest to Susan for trade if need be.  He kept what little foodstuffs that were in the saddle bags along with the two black powder rifles.  The bloody clothing had soaked in the stream all night and since none would fit him, he gave everything to the females to either wear or trade.

Susan insisted he keep half of the coinage and paper money that was on the bodies.  The paper money was from three different banks in Missouri and Kansas and the coinage was very old, dating back into the 21st Century, before the war.

Willem had never fired a gun before but had seen them and knew how they functioned.  One of the two he now had was still loaded so he tied it to a tree and fired it with a long string attached to the trigger.  He had examined the gun powder that he had taken off the outlaws and it seemed extremely coarse.  Willem had tied a piece of canvas between two trees about twenty yards from the muzzle and examined it after firing the rifle.  There were burn spots on the canvas from burning powder bits.  He just loaded the rifles onto the travois and decided to wait until he found a quiet place to experiment with the rifles and powder.

As he rode west, Willem considered something the old man had taught him when he was younger while learning how to forge steel into tools. The old man had taken a small amount of flour and tossed it into the air letting it form a small, powdery cloud then put a burning stick into the middle of the cloud. The flour acted like it exploded in mid-air. Willem had a small mortar and pedestal for grinding up dried herbs made from polished limestone. He would grind a portion of the black powder to a much finer grain and experiment on how it burned and effected the performance of the rifles. He also knew he could blow himself up if he mishandled the powder charge in these crude rifles.

# Lake Side

A week later Willem found his path blocked by a large lake which if he was correct, it was the Grand Lake of the Cherokee's in Oklahoma. Now he had to travel north to get around the lake which made him consider what Susan had told him about going to Coffeyville from Cassville. Her husband should have taken a different route than he had taken which made Willem think about what he had not been told during their short time together. It wasn't that it was his problem concerning the relationship between Susan and her husband but what lay ahead as he traveled north?

Willem found a nice, secluded spot near the lake to camp for a few days to fish and smoke the fish for traveling. From the remains of old boat docks and boats lying well in shore from the water's edge, Willem estimated that the dams which had formed this lake had partially failed allowing the lake level to fall over two hundred feet from where the docks and boats were in ruins.

This also gave him the chance to test his theory on the gun powder. He first took a pinch of gun powder and burned it to see the color of the flame then he ground some to about half the granular size and burned it. The color was richer, and it burned much faster. Here is where the old man's teachings were paying off. The old man may have worked him like a mule during the day, lifting and carrying everything from rocks to steel around the forge but he also took time to explain things he often referred to as physics. The evenings and bad weather were used in the cabin learning from the books the old man had as he taught Willem to read and write but most importantly to open the mind to things he might not be able to see but existed in the world just the same.

The old man had taught him languages such as Latin, French and especially Spanish besides what the old man referred to as proper English. He even spent an entire year only allowing Spanish to be spoken unless visitors were present. Over the years the old man would test Willem's language retention by asking a question or giving directions in one language then changing to another language during the discussion.

Willem often wondered how and where the old man was educated but never had the nerve to ask him. He was taught mathematics, language, science, and literature. The old man taught him how to make his own paper to write on and how to make the ink for his quills or how to make a pencil to write with as Willem spent hours learning to not only write a proper sentence but to work out mathematical formulas for a variety of problems or projects. Even the act of making a garden for growing their own food became a problem in Botany and mathematics in determining how large the garden had to be to supply them with enough food to last through a long winter plus the possibility to have a reserve for trade.

He knew he could not safely hold the firearm and test his theory on the powder, so Willem built a frame to support the rifle in a level configuration. Willem also understood recoil from shooting a bow and used a stiff but bendable sapling to hold the butt of the rifle in place. It took some doing but he rigged up a recoil indicator which would show how far the rifle had moved backwards before the sapling pushed it back into firing position.

Besides fishing to replenish his food supply, Willem had taken a deer for red meat. At fifty paces from the muzzle of the rifle he stretched the deer hide between two trees and marked it with a piece of charcoal as an aim point. To save the lead bullets, he carved hardwood to fit the bullet diameter and since wood is lighter than lead, he had to make them long to simulate bullet weight.

Willem was always concerned with being discovered by unsavory elements but the smoke from his fires generally went out over the lake which helped conceal his location. He didn't know how to muffle the firing of the rifles during his testing but hoped he could find an answer quick enough not to bring guests to his location. Willem made a simple powder measuring device from wood giving him the ability to make it deeper if he had too. The weight of the bullet was determined by constructing a simple beam scale. A lead bullet one side against his wooden bullets on the other. He knew it was not perfect, but he would whittle away the long-wooded bullet until he was close to weight. He insured both ends of the wooden bullet were of proper diameter, so it would not bind up going in or coming out.

It took nearly three days of work before he was ready for his first test. The first shot showed very little recoil and he had seen the wooden bullet hit the ground well in front of the target. He kept increasing the powder until he was hitting the target within a hands width of his mark. His next test was how well would an actual bullet fly.

He fired the first lead bullet from the stand and was moderately pleased with the results. The bullet had impacted six inches high and two inches to the right of his mark. Willem removed the rifle from the stand and fired it from his shoulder as he steadied the rifle against a tree. The bullet hit closer this time and in two more tests it came within inches of the other bullets. Willem understood these rifles were not real accurate but would do the job if the target was big enough. He stepped back, doubling his range and found the bullet strike was close enough to his two-inch black target dot if he had been shooting as a deer, he would have killed it.

Willem ground all the powder to the same consistency and found he now had enough powder for approximately two hundred shots. These rifles used percussion caps which he had seventy-three left after testing but his lead bullet count was only forty-eight after he had test fired both rifles. One of the outlaws did have a small steel pot with a dipper and bullet mold in his saddle bags. Now all Willem needed to do was find a source of lead to cast his own bullets then a place to obtain more percussion caps.

In the three weeks Willem stayed in the lake area, he greatly supplemented his supply of smoked meats and hides. In moving along this shore on foot while hunting with his bow, he found vegetables growing wild near the ruins of old homes. He carefully searched these ruins for anything he might be able to use. In one he found a block of salt with the paper container rotting away from it. It had one time been ground and loose, but moisture had caused it to form into a rock like consistency. He took it back to his camp and broke it up then ground the pieces to once more into a granular form as needed.

When he found eating utensils marked with an 'SS' on them he knew they were stainless steel and could be cleaned up for use or trade. Nick knacks made from lead or pewter were a prize since he could melt them down for bullets. In one old home that was partially burned, he found silver artifacts that he could also melt down for bullets or to make simple coins for trade. Willem returned to this house with all his belongings and spent two days going through the ruins finding tools that had not rusted beyond repair and items of value to trade.

His travois was becoming close to being overloaded at this point, so he looked around the ruins for anything that might make a larger, sturdier travois. Across the top of a wire fence at one home were long, thin walled pipe which was longer than the arms of his own travois. Willem smiled as he remembered the remains of a small, horse drawn wagon at another house that had metal wheels.

It took two days for Willem to fashion a new travois out of the metal pipe and fastening the wheels with their metal axle to the framework.  He had two of the tubes on a side to hopefully strengthen it from the weight and fastened the axle to a point that would place the most weight on them and not on the horse.

Willem heated pig fat until it was liquid and poured it over the axle at the wheels to help loosen them from the rust and soon they spun on the axle.  He loaded the new travois with all he felt he needed and that the horse could deal with and set off on the next part of his journey.  He was pleased that the wheels kept the travois high enough off the ground to avoid dragging it over some of the obstacles in his path.

# Civilization?

As he moved north to Kansas, he would take a few minutes to examine any abandoned houses he came too. He had a small optical magnifier that the old man had which gave him the ability to look further than his eyesight would allow but in one house he found a pair of binoculars that had survived without rusting up or clouding the optics. The leather strap had rotted away but he easily fixed that and wore them around his neck while riding. He worked in the evenings cutting tanned hides to make a scabbard for one of the rifles as he laid the other across his saddle for quick use if needed.

The maps he was using on his journey did not give him the terrain definition as did the map he learned to read and navigate with, but that map was of the area around the cabin. Once more he used what road signs he could find or towns he could identify as he turned west for Coffeyville. One thing about the Kansas map that he only understood as the old man had explained it. Kansas City, Topeka, and Wichita were all circled in red with an 'X' in it. Several of the maps had cities marked that way and the old man only told him they had been destroyed in the war and were dangerous to enter.

It was late summer now and Willem was only wearing an open buckskin vest as he sat on a ridge watching people move around in the part of Coffeyville he could see. He had been sitting there for two days watching and listening for violence. People moved in and out of town at will with wagons hauling everything from wheat to fire wood.

During the trip to Coffeyville, Willem had melted down all the silver and cast them using the bullet mold. He had sixty-eight silver bullets in a separate bag along with seventeen gold bullets in a smaller bag. This did not include the gold and silver coinage the old man had put away over the years that he had brought with him.

Early the next morning Willem rode off the ridge towards Coffeyville with hopes that they would accept him as nothing more than a traveler. His entrance into Coffeyville did draw some attention but for the most part people acted as if his presence was normal. He was well into town when he spotted a sign announcing Markham's General Store. Willem rode up to the store and tied his horse to the rail there and checked to insure the horse pulling the travois was secure to his saddle. The fact he was carrying a rifle did not seem to bother anyone since nearly everyone in town was also carrying some form of firearm.

Walking into the general store was like walking into another world. The smells of herbs and spices along with a musty odor he could not identify. But he could also smell oil such as the old man often used to lubricate the metal parts of the tools he used to form some of the things he built in the forge. Willem noticed a sign behind one of the counters and walked over to read it. On it was the exchange rate for gold and silver by the ounce which made

Willem smile to himself since it was far higher than some of the prices written on cards displayed with various items in the store.

An older man with greying hair walked down the counter and introduced himself.

"I don't think I've ever seen you in here before. My name is Clyde Markham."

"I'm Willem. Do you have a manner of weighting gold and silver?"

"Sure do. It's down at the end of the counter."

Willem reached into the silver pouch and retrieved one of the silver bullets and showed it to Markham.

"Let's see what this is worth if you have time."

"Is that silver?"

"Yes Sir, I was running low of lead when I cast it and a few others."

They walked back to the apothecary scale sitting on the counter. Willem smiled because he had one just like it on the travois but had refrained from unpacking it because he understood it needed a steady, windless area to properly work. But he had taken a one-ounce weight from it as he packed the travois this morning just in case he needed to test the trustworthiness of the people he would be dealing with.

"Well Willem let's see what that musket ball is worth. I will need to test it to insure it is silver. No offense meant to you."

"None taken as I would also want to test it, but let me test your scale first."

Willem held out the one-ounce weight which caused Markham to laugh.

"It looks like you are familiar with weights and scales. Sure, let us check the scale to insure neither of us get cheated."

Markham took the weight from Willem and placed it on one tray then looked at his own weights to find a one-ounce weight. Once both trays had weights in them, Markham unlocked the scale and even though it waiver at unlocking it settled to show that both weights matched. Markham took Willem's weight off and handed it back to him then Willem handed him the bullet. It weighted one and three-quarters ounce. Markham took a small bottle of acid from under the counter and dropped a single drop on the bullet and watched how it reacted.

"Willem, I judge this to be pure silver. When you cast it did you skim off the impurities?"

"Yes Sir, I did. Now we know the weight of one, shall we do some shopping and we can settle up afterwards."

"Willem. Excuse me but do you have a last name?"

"No Sir, and never had one. It was never needed back in the Ozarks in Missouri."

"You don't sound like someone from the Ozarks, and we have had several pass through here over the years."

"My guardian demanded what he called proper English and it is now a habit. So, let me look around a bit then we can get down to business."

Willem bought ten pounds of beans and ten pounds of rice in cloth bags along with twenty pounds of salt. Markham asked him why so much salt, and Willem said he would use it to salt down meat during his travel to preserve it. Willem was very selective in his purchases as he bought a half pound of black pepper plus a grinder to use with it. Markham told him nearly everything came from back east by a monthly freight wagon.

One thing that interested Willem was a glass case with firearms in it. Handguns to be exact. Behind that was a rack with rifles standing up in it. All the rifles had a lever to operate it. Markham said they also came from back east and they were patterned off the old Winchesters from the 19th and early 20th Century. The pistols were patterned after the 1873 Colt Single Action Army pistol the old cavalry used to fight the Indians and keep the peace. Both the rifles and the pistols fired the old 45 Colt cartridge. The rifles came in two lengths of barrels. The short one was called a carbine and the long one a rifle. Willem asked to handle both as he stood his black powder rifle against the counter. Engraved on the side of the receiver was the words Model 1873.

Willem chose the rifle over the carbine because of the longer tubular magazine and based on what he had learned the longer barrel should be more accurate. He decided on buying the rifle and a pistol since the black powder rifles were good for only one shot and as quick as he was with his bow, he would never be that quick if confronted by more than one man with firearms.

Markham outfitted him with a cartridge belt and holster. Willem had to shift the knife he carried on his right hip to the left, so it would not get in the way of the pistol. He also bought six boxes of cartridges since he knew he had to practice with both firearms once he cleared Coffeyville. Markham offered to buy his black powder rifles, but Willem decided to hang onto them for hunting but did buy more lead bullets and percussion caps to make up the difference in the amount of powder he had available.

Willem paid with the silver bullets and told Markham not to worry about the left-over money. Markham tossed in five pounds of beef jerky to make up the difference then offered to exchange the rest of the silver bullets for actual silver and gold coinage. Willem knew the exchange between silver and gold would change from town to town, but the coins would be at face value. He made the exchange without concern knowing what he had in reserve.

As Markham was weighting and insuring the weights were correct, Willem tried on a couple wide brimmed hats to wear on the trail. He had already bought a couple flannel shirts plus a rain slicker to wear instead of his buckskin poncho. Markham helped him put his new purchases on his travois with the black powder rifle also joining the other rifle on the travois. Most of the beef jerky went into the saddlebags along with the boxes of cartridges.

Willem walked back into the store and picked up a box of hard rock candy then rolled a silver bullet across the counter to Markham and smiled before turning away and walking out the door without waiting for change. Markham came out to watch Willem leave and Willem just touched the brim of his new light grey felt hat then gently urged the horses out onto the street and headed out of town as he sucked on a single piece of candy.

He noticed as he rode out of town people seemed to pay him more attention. He took his time eating a piece of jerky for his noon meal as he wanted as much distance between him and Coffeyville as possible before he left the road and once again moved off the beaten path. Willem watched the sun and moved to the south of the road into a gathering of trees and made camp for the night.

Tonight, Willem pitched his tent in an 'A' frame mode instead of a lean too. Once the fire had waned, he crawled into the tent then crawled out the back into the darkness. He left his new rifle in the tent but had his bow and quiver positioned where he could retrieve it as he crawled further into the darkness. Willem had test fired both the rifle and pistol before fixing the evening meal and was surprised at the accuracy of both but felt they both needed a bit of fine tuning, especially the removal of rough edges on the trigger mechanism.

There was a half-moon tonight and the fire was just high enough to give Willem a good view of his tent and surrounding area. It was some time before he first heard the rustling of dry leaves of the men who were approaching his camp. Willem had his quiver placed so he could just reach down and pull a fresh arrow without fumbling with things and had one already to pull back if needed.

The men slowly approached the camp and spread out with the small fire between them and the tent. As if a practiced move, all three of them raised their rifle and then began shooting into the tent. Willem released his first arrow at the most distance man and never looked to see if it impacted his target as he was taking his next shot. Once more the years of training the old man had insisted on played in his favor as his ambushers died in short order with a long shaft arrow through their chests.

Willem quickly moved from his location towards the direction the men had come from. Were they alone or was there someone holding their horses? Willem had never worn boots, but wore calf high buckskin moccasins with the soles made from the hide of an Arkansas Razorback hog. He had been stalking game since he was five and could move through the thickest layer of leaves without hardly a sound. He found the horses roughly three hundred paces from his camp tied to the scrub. Only three horses and he had not heard a single sound to indicate another rider had ridden off.

He gathered the horses and took them back to his camp. At the camp he quickly went through the men's pockets only taking those things he could use which amounted to a small amount of coinage. Willem also went through the saddlebags of the men and once more only took those things he could use. Weapons and knives went into a pile along with the ammunition for them. He lifted each body onto a horse and tied it, so it would not fall off then broke camp loading the men's things onto his travois.

Willem took one of his precious pieces of homemade paper and made a note which he attached to one of the bodies.

"My name is Willem and I mean no harm as I travel west. These men tried to kill me and take what was mine. Do not follow me or you will suffer their fate. I travel with no malice towards men and will not tolerate malice towards my person."

He took all the horses out to the old road and headed the horses with the bodies towards Coffeyville and slapped them on their way before mounting his own horse and riding away from this location.

Willem knew the smart thing to do was to use the other horses to carry the load the travois was carrying as it was showing the strain of being close to overweight in its burden, but it would have taken him at least a day to balance the loads between horses and he was not going to waste the time. Maybe he could buy another horse or two further west with the money he had.

As he rode in the darkness Willem considered the cost of this journey. He had killed eight men who were intent on evil. His mind went to young Martha and her rape. Would she recover or be broken inside for the rest of her life? Susan? The way she had acted, he could have taken her body that night and doubted she would have fought him since they both knew that her rapists would have most likely killed her and Martha once they had their fill of them.

The old man had made him read a book only titled 'The Holy Bible'. He had told Willem that it was the history of the Jewish race during the early times of men. Some considered it to be righteous while others considered it mythology. Regardless, there were stories within which could guide a person in life. It did not matter if one believed the book to be truthful, but the moral teachings were important when dealing with others.

'Do unto others as you would have them do unto you.' Those men came to him to do him harm and he gave them what they intended for him. There was a certain twinge of guilt in killing those men, but they chose the path they walked and even if there was no god in the heavens to judge him for his actions, he felt he would pass the test needed to pass through to the other side if it existed.

Willem put this out of his mind and just let his horse take him west as he rested as best he could in the saddle.

# On The Prairie

Willem had ridden well past mid-day before finding a place to camp and rest up from the long night. No one came after him for the killing of the men and he moved out of this camp at daylight to put as many miles as he could between him and Coffeyville.

Almost two weeks later he found an abandoned farm house on what he figured was Bluff Creek just west of the ghost town bearing the name Bluff City. The house was in shambles, but the two metal barns were still standing. Inside one of the barns Willem found an old Ferrier's forge with a hand crank blower to help heat the metal. There was also a large anvil and tools.

When he found the farm, he noticed that there were no indications of movement around the place except for the small trails animals often made. The weather would soon turn colder, and he considered this to be a place he could camp for the winter. He had bought more supplies back in the town of South Haven Kansas and could make the trip back there with only his horse in a day if needed. Plus, there was an old wagon for a single horse to pull that he might be able to repair if given the time and he could find everything he would need around this farm. It had used the old rubber wheels, but they had long since rotted away. Willem put his mind to considering how to convert the rims using wood and metal bands such as he helped the old man make many times back in Missouri.

It took Willem several days to clean out the one barn especially pulling the old tractor out of it. He sat in the tractor's seat for nearly an hour messing with the controls until he figured out to put one lever in the middle or neutral position which allowed him to pull the tractor from the barn with the horses. He was able to pull the old wagon into the barn and went to work on it.

He turned the horses out into a fenced area with a pond on it after checking and repairing the barbed wire fence with wire taken from other fences. Wood taken from the farm house was used to repair the rotted wagon wood and it took him hours to remove the old, metal rims from the axles then cut the remains of the rubber tires from them. Willem looked under debris in the other barn for anything he could use and found a metal can with grease that has thickened but he felt was still useable.

Willem had very little time for anything except work as he not only worked to repair the wagon but hunted for game at the same time he build a smoker from bricks from the old farm house. He used his bow or black powder rifles more often than his new firearms in gathering meat to save what ammunition he had in case he could not locate a source for more cartridges. Willem had disassembled his pistol and rifle, deburring the rough edges of the firing mechanism and actions. The weapons he took from the men he had killed were like the ones he had bought and did the same with them.

His pistol belt now had his twelve-inch bladed knife attached on the left along with a holster sitting tilted, so he could reach across his waist and draw it while riding besides the holster with his new pistol hanging on his right side and tied down on his leg. He now had two rifles in scabbards attached to his saddle when riding plus a looped belt hanging from his saddle horn with fifty cartridges if needed beyond what was on his actual belt.

Willem had brought four black bear hides with him from Missouri and made a heavy coat to protect him from the cold wind and rain here on the prairie.

He had been at the farm for over a month when he decided he needed to go back to South Haven and purchase supplies. Willem was pulling his travois behind his horse, leaving the other one at the farm so he could travel faster. Prices were higher in South Haven than in Coffeyville plus the exchange rate for silver and gold was lower which told Willem the people here were making a nice profit on the exchange.

Willem spent the night in the stables in town and left before daylight. It had started snowing before dark and he did not want to be caught out in the open during the night. As he had entered the town he passed a family with a wagon heading west out of town. It was mid-day and the snow was beginning to blow harder when he came upon the family huddled next to the wagon with a broken wheel just outside of Bluff City.

The family was huddled under several quilts trying to stay warm, but the father was missing. It was only the mother, a daughter and a younger son.

"Where is your husband?"

"He went back to South Haven for help."

Willem knew if he had made it to South Haven he would have gone to the stables since he could have obtained a wagon and help there. In this cold weather Willem figured he passed the husbands body somewhere along the road. He looked at the wheel and knew he could fix it back at the farm but not out here in the open.

"Ma'am I just left South Haven this morning and no one came in needing help. I'm sorry but I think the cold got your husband. We're not that far from Bluff City and can find shelter there. But we need to get moving before the weather worsens."

Willem put the woman and the young boy on his horse wrapping them up with a couple quilts then had the girl sit on his travois and covered her with another quilt. He took the reins and began to walk towards Bluff City leading the horse and their horse that he had unhitched from the wagon.

He found a building that could provide protection from the weather and built a fire on the concrete floor. Willem had brought both horses into the building to protect them and used the small pot he carried in his saddlebags to melt snow for drinking water and to warm the survivors from the inside out.

After he had warmed up a bit he told them to just stay where they were and keep the fire going but do not let it burn too high in order not to set the building on fire. He then went from building to building finding things he could use to close the shelter more, and to give them something to sit or lie on without being on the hard, cold concrete. Willem also found a couple larger stainless-steel pots and pans at an old diner and brought them back to the shelter where he scrubbed them hard with dirt to clean them before sitting them on the fire filled with snow to melt for cooking some of the beans he had bought the day before. As the water was heating up he went back and found some china bowels and silverware to eat with. He cleaned them as he did the pots and washed them in some of the heated water as the beans were cooking.

It was over the hot food that he introduced himself.

"My name is Willem. Yours?"

The woman said her name was Gloria and the girl's name was Linda. The boy was called Mike and they were heading for Garden City to work a farm her husband's brother had out there.

Gloria told him that everything they owned was on that wagon including a box with what little money they had. The building had warmed around the fire and soon the family went to sleep while Willem watched over them keeping the fire going until he finally laid down and rested.

Willem was awakened by the sound of Gloria scrapping one of the pots across the concrete floor as she put it on the fire that she had built up. Willem got up and went back into the building and relieved his bladder. When he turned to go back to the fire, Gloria was standing there looking at him.

"Willem, are you certain my husband Henry is dead?"

"No Gloria I cannot be completely certain but in that snow if he lost his bearings and mistakenly left the road, he could not have survived the cold. After I get some food in me, I'm going back after your wagon. With two horses I think I can drag it into town."

"Thank you, Willem, for all you have done."

"Gloria, it was the proper thing to do. I need no thanks."

She just nodded and turned away to lead him back to the campfire. Willem left soon after eating but asked Gloria if she knew how to use a handgun. She said she did and he took the spare he carried in his saddlebag and handed it to her. He looked at the girl and in this light, she looked older than he thought she was now that she was not bundled up. She gave him a weak smile and he nodded then gathered the horses and left.

By the time he got to the wagon the snow had let up but was blowing across the open prairie. Willem was grateful for the bearskin coat he was wearing and had even made boots from it. But the wind was still biting through to his skin. His gloves were bulky, and he had to remove them to make sure of the final hitching of the horses to the wagon. The snow-covered road helped to pull the wagon as it skidded on the snow as he led the horses instead of riding one of them.

Willem brought the wagon to the back side of the building and unfastened the horses to get them inside out of the cold wind. Gloria had hot beans on the edge of the fire and he ate a bowl full before going back out and cutting grass for the horses to eat.

The children were moving about the building when he returned gathering up bits of wood and anything else that would burn for the fire. Willem hated to see the old books set aside for the fire but for one survival meant more than they did plus after decades of neglect, the pages were nearly glued together making them unreadable. Gloria went to the wagon and brought back a skillet and salt pork which she cooked for dinner to go with the beans. She also brought in a tin of tea and boiled some to drink. Willem told the family he was going to take them to his place in the morning and to get as much rest as possible this night.

Neither the girl nor the boy had said much around Willem but when he pulled out some hard candy from his saddlebag after the evening meal both thanked him and the girl, Linda gave him a nice smile.

Willem was lucky the next morning in that the snow had stopped and the sun had come out, but the wind still had a bitter bite to it against exposed skin. He hooked his travois to the back of the wagon and had the family sit close together under several quilts as he led the horses on foot. If there had been a wagon jack available, he would have fixed a piece of timber under axle to lift and provide a skid to ride on but without one that was impossible. It was well past mid-day when he pulled wagon into the barn he was staying in and had to unhitch the horses then his travois before he could close the barn doors and close off the wind.

His first task was to get a fire lit in the fire pit he had constructed using brick from the farm house in anticipation of the cold weather then tend to the horses including checking on the horse he had left behind. Willem had worked hard in the previous weeks finding and closing gaps in the metal and such to keep out the wind and the wind turbines on the roof had been loosened up which drew the smoke out of the barn. But they also drew out a lot of heat.

Gloria had the kids clean out a couple of stalls for them to live in then went about emptying the wagon of their belongings. In the bottom of the wagon was a metal tub which Gloria said they used to bath in. Another stall was cleaned out and the tub placed in it. Canvas they had in the wagon was hung around the stall to provide privacy and Willem built a small fire pit to heat this area and to heat water on for bathing. Once the wagon was empty, everyone helped Willem as he pushed it back outside the barn to give them more room to move around.

It took several hours before it became warm enough in the barn to remove the heavy clothing each were wearing, and Willem did not miss the fact that the girl was older then he first thought. Willem had labored long hours cutting the tall grass and hauling it into the barn to feed the horses over the winter. He now put some in each stall to make a bed on.

Before he had left for South Haven, Willem had killed a small deer and had it hanging at the far end of the barn away from the fire pits. Gloria cut off several steaks and cooked them up for the evening meal along with making drop biscuits. She told Willem that she along with Linda would take care of the cooking and such freeing him to do the things he needed to do and when possible, Mike would help even though he was only eleven. It was during this conversation he found out that Linda was seventeen.

The next few days were taken up with gathering more wood from the old farmhouse to burn for heat and cooking. Willem also rigged up a way to get rid of the water from the bath tub without having to go outside. It was crude but would work.

46

The family bathed the next day and Willem checked to make sure the disposal system worked well enough.

It was nearly two weeks later while Willem was just sitting in the hot water enjoying the heat on his tired body when Linda entered the bathing stall and removed her clothing before stepping into the tub with him.

"Willem before you say anything, I've been with a man before and mom knows about that. She also knows I was going to come in here with you. If you don't want me, I'll understand."

Willem never spoke, he just pulled her to him and kissed her. He had turned twenty-one a month before and seventeen was not too young for a girl to be with a man. Back in Missouri he knew of several girls that were married and with children by Linda's age. They washed each other and when done, Linda mounted him in the tub. She made no attempt to remain quiet as they enjoyed their coupling. After they dried each other off, she went to his stall and joined him on his pallet.

Linda had been sleeping with Willem for almost two weeks when the weather broke, and a short period of thaw began. He saddled up his horse and left to go back to South Haven to obtain more supplies, and to look for Gloria's husband.

About an hour out of South Haven, Willem noticed a mound of snow that seemed out of place. He found Gloria's husband beneath the snow, frozen in death. He went on into South

Haven and purchased the things on the list he and Gloria had worked out. She had given him half of their meager funds to help pay for the supplies. On the return trip, he placed the body in a piece of canvas he had brought with him, and drug it behind the horse back to the farm.

It took most of the next day for Willem to dig a grave in the frozen ground for the body. Gloria had looked at the body to insure it was her husband before going through all his pockets to remove his meager property before burial. She tried to give Willem his pocket watch, but Willem told her he had one in his things that had belonged to the old man that had raised him, besides it should go to Mike, his son.

Another storm hit a few days later but Willem had taken advantage of the break to hunt and had two more deer and a hog hanging in the barn. He had purchased more than enough beans and flour to get them through the rest of the winter plus tea. The spices he had bought helped with the flavor of the foods, so they did not become too boring.

Linda did not come to his bed every night which was not a big thing for Willem, but a month after they had buried Gloria's husband, she came to his bed. Willem never put any demands on either female and never asked them to come to his bed. They came to him when they desired, and he did all he could to satisfy them while there.

Mike helped Willem daily in rebuilding the other wagon and getting it ready for the trip west. He never commented on his mother or sister spending nights with Willem. He did pay close attention to everything Willem was doing and often asked questions concerning the rebuild. Willem became a teacher and took his time to answer each question asked of him. He considered Mike to be brighter than he often let on and absorbed the information Willem was providing him. If Willem asked Mike a question a week later about something he had asked Willem, he almost always answered it clear enough that Willem knew he had learned the lesson well.

As the weather broke and spring was weeks away, the women began wearing less clothing to stay warm inside the barn. Linda took him into his stall one afternoon and just raised her dress to him. That night Gloria came to his bed. He had told them once the ground had dried enough, they were leaving, and he would see them safely to Garden City before going on to Colorado and the mountains.

Willem had not only fixed their wagon wheel, he had built a spare in case of need. Using metal rims he had found in the other barn that fit his wagon, he made two extra wheels. Besides the wagon jack he had found in the barns he had also found two scissor jacks that once soaked in the oil from the tractor's engine, had loosened up and would work for his needs.

He took the wagon out for a test of the wheels he had built and had to do a minor repair on one before he was satisfied with his work. He silently thanked the old man for teaching him how to work both metal and wood.

Willem dismounted the anvil from its concrete pedestal and with a lot of effort placed it in the back of his wagon along with a large vise that he had taken nearly a week to loosen up from the rust built up on it. He put the Ferrier's forge in the wagon and hoped his reinforcement of the wagon's bed would handle the weight.

Both wagons were loaded the night before they were to leave with everything except what they would need for the morning meal. Willem had made one last trip to South Haven for supplies two days before and based upon the distance he could gage on the map, they would have enough food to get to Garden City and some to spare.

While stripping the old farm house for wood they had found several items made of silver which Willem melted down for use as exchange once more casting them into bullets, but even with the new castings, he had expended over half his funds during his stay at the farm. Every time Gloria had given him some of her funds to buy food, he just tucked it away, saving it for her once they reached Garden City.

The trip to Garden City was without incident as Linda drove his wagon and Gloria drove theirs while he rode his horse to be free in case of trouble. Each night on the road presented Willem with a bed mate of one or the other of the females.

When they reached Garden City, Willem gave Mike the pouch he had been saving Gloria's money in and told him to give it to her once he had left town. Supplies were thin and costly in Garden City after the harsh winter, but Willem stocked up as best he could and spent one last night with Linda before he left them in the company of her brother-in-law. He knew enough about females to know that both had stopped having their menstruation cycles which meant he was probably leaving them both pregnant with his child.

Willem knew that regardless of the situation with the females, he had to continue with his journey, and the risk of taking either or both females was too great to consider. The women never commented on their condition and he pretended it did not matter. Silently he promised himself if his destiny gave him the means, he would return to collect the women and his children, so he could properly attend to his responsibilities. He did leave a gold bullet with each woman and told them to get proper value from them.

# Crossing the Rockies

Willem entered the town of Pueblo Colorado nearly a month after leaving Garden City. He had given a rifle to Mike along with a box of cartridges and sold the rest of the extra firearms in Pueblo to help pay for the supplies he would need to cross the mountains ahead of him. He had the means of paying for everything, but he also figured he did not need so many firearms.

He sought out the local sheriff and talked to him about the best passage over the mountains. Willem told the sheriff he was headed to Montrose Colorado to meet up with his brother who was starting a ranch out there. The truth was he was heading further than that. He was headed to Utah and a place already marked on his map of that state. But the old man had told him to never tell anyone where he was headed but never explained why.

The sheriff gave him the best passage he felt would be the easiest to traverse but suggested that he use both horses to pull the wagon. Willem spent the next two days working with the local stable master reconfiguring his wagon for two horses and bought another horse, so he could keep his horse free if needed or he had to replace one because of wear on the horse or accident.

The road was well marked and used by freight wagons going back and forth over the mountains. Here he got lucky and joined up with five other wagons, one being a cook's wagon, that were heading over the mountains hauling freight to Grand

Junction. Willem had changed out of his buck skins into denim trousers and regular boots. The boots felt funny on his feet after two decades of wearing moccasins, but he quickly adjusted to them.

One of the teamsters he was traveling with made fun of Willem's two-gun rig until one evening while sitting around the cook's fire Willem drew the pistol from his cross draw and shot a rattlesnake near another teamster's foot. No one commented about his revolvers after that. Willem also would turn over his wagon to one of the extra teamsters and go off on his horse to hunt for fresh meat, normally in the form of an elk. A week into the trip, the teamsters became very friendly with Willem and took care of his things while he was off hunting.

When one of the teamster's horses threw a shoe, Willem took the anvil and forge off his wagon, so he could form a new shoe from the blanks he had taken from the farm he had wintered in. Once finished, the teamsters offered to put the anvil back in the wagon, but it took two of them when he had done it by himself. They developed a new respect for him because of his strength.

Willem left the wagon train at Montrose with nearly all his food supplies since the wagon trains cook had told him as long as he provided fresh meat to the train, he could save his own rations and they would share theirs with him since they always carried more than the needed in case they had to stop for a time to fix a broken wagon.

It had been three months since he had left the women in Garden City when he turned west for Utah. It would be two more weeks before he crossed into Utah.

# The Place is Haunted

Eight days after crossing into Utah, Willem found himself in the town of Green River Utah. The people were somewhat stand-offish, and there was not much to the town. When they found out where he was heading, they warned him to avoid that area. He had told them he was going to head southwest and was heading for Arizona. The sheriff advised him not to go that route since that area was haunted.

The sheriff claimed people went into that region but were never heard from again. When Willem asked if they were travelers, how would he know if they were lost forever? The sheriff said hunters had gone in there to hunt buffalo and never came back. No one suggested anything except to change his route directly south, or turn back and go home.

Willem spent the next six days at the edge of town, restocking and rearranging his wagon for the next part of his trip. This also gave his horses a chance to rest and eat their fill of the grass that was growing there. Also, this gave him a chance to eat at a place in town for a change, and conserve his own rations.

It was at this eatery that he drew the attention of an older woman who waited the tables. Late on the second night, after the eatery closed, she came to his camp. When he hesitated to take her to his bed under the canvas lean-to by the wagon, she told him she was barren and not to concern himself with the possibility of bringing a child into the world with her.

Darlene was her name and she came to him every night he was camped there, always leaving soon afterwards to return to her lodgings. She was very physical with Willem and even preformed with her mouth, unlike others he had bedded. The last night she came to him, she took him complete with her mouth, then later aroused him again with her mouth before he took her beneath him. He lay on his pallet after she left and could only smile at the enjoyment she had given him as he pondered if other women took men in that fashion.

Willem left Green River heading due south for three days before turning back on the path his map said he needed to go. The metal box the old man said contained his destiny now resided in a shoulder bag that was always slung over his shoulder, or next to him when he bedded down for the night.

Just before he stopped for the night, he came across a group of travelers who were coming up from Arizona. He pitched camp with them since they were two families moving north to escape the heat and to find greener pastures for the cattle they were bringing with them.

They told him a like story about the haunted area in the direction Willem was headed and that they had come close to the area several times during their passage. They told of hearing strange sounds during the day and night, but the sounds were not bad enough to spook the cattle.

Within this group was the daughter of one of the couples and she took notice of Willem. She had red hair and was every bit as attractive as Linda, maybe more so, but she was only fifteen seasons old. Willem turned any thoughts about her inside and tried not to admire her as she moved about the camp, tending to those things her mother had her deal with.

She did come to him later, but Willem was able to send her away without hurting her feelings. As Willem was lying on his pallet, considering how far he had come, one of the women crawled under his lean-to and offered herself to him. He had not given her any consideration since she had a wedding ring on her hand, but she told him she was a widow, and the sister to the head of the group. She just wanted the closeness of a man, and left his bed soon after she recovered from their coupling.

Nine days out of Green River, Willem heard a whirling sound for the first time. He looked for where the sound was coming from but could never seem to locate the source. It came and went at odd times during the day and night. Willem had no idea what could cause the sound but the ghosts he had been warned about knew exactly what it was.

The drone operator sat watching the monitor as he maneuvered the small drone to get closer photos of the male subject driving the wagon with odd looking wheels towards their outer perimeter. The computers had given him a basic outline of the man's physical form but the one thing that had his supervisors interested in this man was his blond hair. Blond hair was not rare within the community, but it was very rare for an outsider to have blond hair.

They had four good photos of him to include one taken two evenings before as he was stripped naked washing himself. The operator took the last photo before packaging them to be sent to the council that had request more data on the man. Usually intruders into the outer perimeter were scared off or if they persisted, removed in order not to be a threat to the community. Some had their memories erased and taken to Arizona and released with memories of another life. Only in rare cases were they killed to preserve the secret of the community.

Julia Malkin looked at the photos of this newest intruder and had to admire his physical form. She was the head of security for the community and currently between lovers. She noticed that this individual always had a bag over his shoulder or it was within reach as was a handgun even if he was cleaning his body. They had a video of him stalking one of the many deer in the area and she had watched how he moved during the stalk.

Unlike others she had watched, this man moved gracefully in the stalk and drew as close as possible before making the kill. His aim was true, and the deer fell where it was standing. She watched as he gutted and then picked up the carcass with little difficulty. He wasted no energy in his efforts and she admired him for his abilities. She also wondered what he looked like without the blond beard he wore. But a close-up of his face showed his green eyes and something in the back of her mind said they were not the eyes of one of the barbarians that normally came within their perimeter.

Julia took her report to the council that evening.

"Ladies and Gentlemen, we have a new intruder coming in from the northeast. There is something about this one I cannot classify. If the council approves I would like to bring him in for further study in case the outside world is gaining in a manner which we need to prepare for."

She showed them the photos and the video of this blond headed individual. Julia also pointed out the wheels on his wagon and commented they were far from normal. One overhead photo of the wagon was blown up and showed the anvil which they judged to be over one hundred kilos in weight. Julia then finished the presentation with a photo of the subject standing at the back of the wagon with two books set out as he was going through some of his other things. You could not read the titles of the books from the photo, but they were well preserved, and one had markers in it. This man was educated, and she considered him worth studying.

The council voted to bring him in for study before any action concerning his disposition was to be determined. Julia notified a security team to prepare to go out to bring him and his belongings in.

Surveillance showed that the subject rigged a cover from the wagon to provide cover for the night. The team leader determined that they would take him soon after midnight in order that he would be fully asleep and make capture easier. Julia gave him the go ahead for the capture.

Willem watched the men move on his camp. They were spread out and one nearly stepped on him as he lay in a small depression near the wagon. In the faint moonlight he could tell they were not dressed as the men he had met over the months of travel and their weapons looked odd. He quickly moved on the one who had barely missed stepping over him and knocked him out with a single punch to the back of the head. He caught the falling body and gently laid him down without making any noise.

Willem moved on another man and quickly removed him. Two down, two to go but as they were moving closer to his small fire the risk of detection grew. He took the third man then faded back further into the darkness. He watched the fourth man who suddenly stopped and began to look around for his friends. With the dark clothing the men were wearing they nearly blended into the ground. Willem watched as the only man standing raised his hand up to his face as he backed away from the wagon.

Soon Willem heard the whirling noise again then the lone man turned towards where Willem was crouched. Willem could not see as well as he would have liked but the man seemed to pull something down over his eyes then moved his head back and forth before looking directly at him. The man suddenly pointed his odd weapon at him and Willem rolled out of the way as he heard a slight puffing sound and something metallic hit the rocks behind him.

Willem drew his pistol and fired a single shot which was not aimed at the man but near enough for him to hear the bullet pass his head. Then Willem called out to him.

"I missed you on purpose. The next one will find its mark. Drop your weapon."

The other man shifted his aim and Willem fired again, this time hitting a pouch hanging on the man's left side. This caused the man to pause.

"That one found its mark, the next one will require a doctor. Drop the weapon."

The man laid his weapon down and just stood with his arms out away from his side.

"What about my men?"

"They are alive, but will have a serious headache when they wake up. Now who are you?"

"I'm Captain Lawrence Martin of the Utah Rangers. Who are you?"

"My name is Willem, and I'm just a traveler."

"What's your last name Willem?"

"I have no last name, at least one I have never been told. Why are you here?"

"You're trespassing, and we came to take you into custody."

"Interesting, no one told me that this area was off limits to travelers although I was told this place was haunted. I think I see why now. But understand this Captain Martin, I was instructed to come here by the man that raised me, and I will fulfill his wishes."

As this conversation was occurring, the drone had its directional microphone pointed at Willem picking up his side of the conversation while Captain Martin's was coming in over the radio he wore. Julia was watching from drone control and reached over and the keyed the radio to Martin and asked him for a spelling of Willem's name. When Willem spelled out his name, Julia keyed it into the computer and was shocked at what she saw.

On the monitor was the photo of a tall, blond haired man by the name of Willem Forsyth, one of the primary founders of the community. She quickly split the screen and placed the stranger's photo beside the old one and compared them. Without a DNA test, she was certain this stranger was a direct descendent of one of the founders of the community. She keyed the radio link to the drone.

"Willem, my name is Julia, and Captain Martin works for me. Please holster your firearm. No harm will come to you."

Willem never turned to where the voice was coming from above and behind him as he watched Martin. He slowly holstered the firearm and walked towards Martin. When he was within arm's reach of Martin, he spoke very clearly.

"My mentor, my teacher who sent me on this journey said I would encounter many strange things when I arrived here. Your Julia said no harm would come to me, so you had better hope none does, because you had better pray it ends me, otherwise I will rip you head from your shoulders and beat the next man that gets near me to death with it."

Willem stood a full head over Martin as he spoke, then he turned towards his campfire and the coffee pot of tea at the edge of the fire. He poured a cup, then sat with his back to a wagon wheel noticing that Martin had yet to move from where Willem had left him. Willem suppressed a laugh as he smelled urine coming from where the man was standing.

Julia watched as Willem sat down and sipped on whatever he had poured into the cup.

"Watch Commander, dispatch a Med Team out there now, and get my air car ready, I'm going out there."

Julia was in turmoil inside, because if he was anything like his namesake, he could be the most dangerous man on the planet. And she had to deal with him.

# Paradise City

Willem was leaning back against the wagon wheel looking as if he was asleep except his eyes were not fully closed. The man who called himself Captain Martin had moved about locating his men and checking on their condition but avoided Willem. Just before Willem had laid back he had ejected the two spent cartridges from his revolver and replaced them with fresh ones. He did not holster the weapon but kept it in hand lying across his body as he relaxed and just waited for what he suspected was to occur next.

He heard the air cars long before they arrived. The old man had told him about such things that were common before the war destroyed civilization. He had not been told about this place other than he had to come here and find his destiny. The old man had eluded too many things but was never clear about how he knew of these things. Willem sat and considered that the old man had come from here and possibly so had he before he was old enough to have memories.

They were coming for him now, possibly in force since he had disabled three of the four men that had already been sent. Whomever had sent those men had grossly under estimated him. Now all he had to do was wait.

Suddenly the area was lighted from the sky as the air cars turned on their bright landing lights. One vehicle landed to his left and slightly behind him. Willem heard voices calling out and figured it was some sort of medical team come to recover their injured. Another vehicle landed a modest distance in front of him, far enough out that he was barely pelted by the wind created by the vehicle's fans as it landed.

The lights dimmed to a soft blue and a figure moved out of the darkness into the light as they walked to him. Willem recognized the individual coming to him was female in form and at first, he thought she was nude until she came closer. She was wearing what appeared to be a one-piece body suit with a belt around her waist. She stopped just short of the fire with her hands slightly outward to show him she was not armed.

"Mister Willem, I am Julia Malkin."

Under normal circumstances, Willem would stand in the presence of a female, but tonight he just sat where he was.

"It's just Willem, Miss Malkin. Now why did you send armed men after me in the dark of night, instead of just intercepting me in my travels?"

"Willem, let's just say it was a poor decision without consideration of who you might be?"

"And who might I be Miss Malkin?"

"Do you not know your parentage?"

"No, I only knew the old man who raised and taught me. I never knew his name, and never heard anyone we dealt with call him anything other than old man. But he gave me something that he told me if I come here, someone could unseal it, and within was my destiny."

"What did he give you Willem?"

Willem slowly reached into his shoulder bag with his free hand and removed the small, metal box from it.

"This is what he gave me. The old man taught me how to work steel into tools, but this box is unlike anything he ever taught me."

"Where is this old man now?"

"In a grave in the Ozarks of southern Missouri. Miss Malkin, I have been on the road for over a year. I'm tired, so what is your next move besides boring me with questions?"

"Willem, please surrender your weapons and come with me. I'll take you to our community which I suspect was what the old man wished you to find when he sent you here."

"No. No, I will not surrender my weapons, but I will come with you as long as you can guarantee that my wagon, horses and property are safely transported to that same location."

"Willem, I insist you surrender your firearms."

"Go to hell."

Out of the darkness a loud puff of air as before was heard, and a dart like object struck Willem in the chest. Willem looked at the woman in front of him, and just smiled as he reached up, then pulled it from the leather vest he was wearing. He tossed it into the fire, then calmly pointed his revolver at her.

"You're an attractive woman Julia Malkin, it would be a shame for me to put a bullet hole in you. Tell your men to back off or the next shot might cause my finger to twitch, and cause just that to happen."

"Everyone back away! No more shooting!"

"Very good Miss Malkin. Now, come a bit closer and sit down so we can have a civilized discussion as we wait for daylight."

She moved closer until he finally told her to sit. In the waning light of the campfire, Willem was able to get an even better look at her. Julia was in fact a very attractive woman, but something about her made Willem also consider this was the last woman he would want in his bed. As an animal can sense fear, he could sense fear from her, and it almost seemed he could sense what she was thinking. She was terrified of him and wanted him dead, even though she gave an outward appearance of uncertainty, yet calm.

Julia finally was able to get a clear look at Willem from where she was sitting. His clothing was not what they were familiar with from an outsider. She had to think hard to remember the word for his clothing. Buckskins, made from the softly tanned hide of deer. But this buckskin was stained to break up the pattern and form of the wearer. His blond beard and face was covered in what she suspected was ash from the fire to also help hide him, while his long blond hair was up and covered by dark piece of cloth.

But why didn't the stem dart affect him since it was designed to also go through the hide of an animal and shut it down for capture?

Willem made a point of lowering his handgun to remove part of the threat to her, but it was always in plain sight for her to see. He told her to ask any questions she felt she needed an answer to, and he tried not to be evasive in his answers. Willem was careful in what he asked her as he could sense she was not telling him the whole truth.

The night passed slowly as they talked with him instructing her to put a piece of wood on the fire from time to time and even had her pour him a cup of tea. He offered her a cup, which she refused, but did ask if one of her men could bring her a container of water. The man who brought her water walked slowly and with his hands out to show all he had was the water container then he just turned and walked back into the darkness without speaking.

Julia was feeling exhausted as the adrenalin from being scared and the long hours prior to finding herself sitting next to the campfire were taking their toll on her. The conversation between her and Willem had slowed to a stop which did nothing to help keep her alert. She closed her eyes for a moment and in a moment of clarity, she realized he had more information about her and the community, than she had about him and his presence here. Julia heard a sharp tap of metal on metal and opened her eyes to see Willem smiling at her in the faint rays of dawn.

"Time to wake up Miss Julia and prepare to depart for your community." He softly spoke to her.

She looked down at the chronometer on her wrist and quickly figured she had been dozing for over an hour as she was just sitting upright. Julia had been sitting cross legged and slowly stretched her legs out to remove some of the stiffness from sitting so long in the same position.

"Stand up." Willem instructed.

Julia stood and stretched getting the kinks out of her body. She looked down at him as he smiled at her. Willem noticed that her one-piece coverage was not form fitting, but still it showed she was well endowed in her chest. He sat his tin cup down and stood with the minimum of effort.

Willem still had his revolver in his hand as he stepped close to her. She watched his gun hand closely as he slowly moved it

70

allowing him to holster the revolver back into his cross-draw holster. She had to look up at him since his shoulders were taller than the top of her head. Julia knew he was a large man, but she had never seen one as tall as he was, or been this close to a man as tall as Willem.

"Willem, how tall are you?"

"I'm just under two meters tall. In old English I'm six feet four inches. Why?"

"None of our men are as tall as you. A tall man would maybe be six feet, but he would be rare."

"Then you'll have no problem spotting me in a crowd. It's time to go now."

Willem looked to his right and pointed to one of Julia's men who was kneeling on one knee.

"Come here." He instructed the man.

The man stood and slung his odd-looking rifle behind his back as he walked to Willem. He stopped out of reach and just waited.

"Miss Julia and I are leaving. You will insure all my property will be transported to a location where I can collect it later. Remove nothing, because I know what belongs to me. Also, there are weapons in the wagon that are loaded, so please be careful. Do you understand your instructions?"

"Sir, I'm not a supervisor. You need to give your instructions to a supervisor."

"No Sir, I just gave them to you. You will share those instructions with all who you need to assist you in completing them. I don't need your name because I know your face, and I now hold you responsible for my property. Execute your instructions."

The man looked over at Julia and she nodded it was alright.

"Yes Sir, it will be taken care of."

"Good." He turned back to Julia. "Now we are ready to go. Please lead the way Julia."

Anyone watching from the perimeter of Willem walking towards the air car would think he was completely secure in his person. But he took each step waiting for the sting of a dart in his legs or exposed arms. His limbs were not so much exposed as they were not protected as his torso was. Underneath his buckskins was a layer of buffalo and one of hog hide. These were thick enough to prevent the needles of the darts from penetrating to the skin, but his arms and legs were only protected by the single lay of buckskin he was wearing.

There were two men at the air car, one sitting at the controls and the other standing, holding the passenger compartment door open. The air car was an open topped vehicle with what Willem could determine to be seating for six in the compartment plus two up front. Julia stepped into the car and immediately sat down which would put her on Willem's right. He stopped short of entering and just looked at her. It only took a moment for her to realize what he was thinking and moved over to the far side of the seat. As Willem stepped in, he took the door in hand and closed it behind him, pulling it from the grasp of the man holding it open.

Willem sat down in the spot Julia had just vacated and never looked at the man at the door. Julia suddenly understood that this seating arrangement gave Willem free grasp of his cross-draw pistol, and could cover the entire vehicle without adjusting his seating. She also knew Willem had just prevented her body guard from sitting in the back with them. Julia never looked at Willem or her body guard as he finally took the hint and took a seat in the front.

As the fans came up to speed, Willem did everything he could to relax. He had no idea what the experience of flying would be like, but he was nervous inside. As the air car lifted off, he looked over and could see the Ranger he had told to secure his property talking with four others and pointing to the wagon. Willem was running a bluff and he was worried how long it would last. He had the feeling that these people had never had anyone force their hand in this manner before.

As tempting as it was to look around at the sights passing under the air car, Willem stayed focused on the people in the car. He looked over at Julia and as calm as she seemed, she was gripping her hands in a manner showing she feared what was happening and she had no control over the events taking place. If as she said she was in charge of these Rangers, then he had her right where he wanted her. But he also remembered that scared people are often the most dangerous because they are unpredictable in their actions.

Willem knew how to tell time with a watch, but the old man's watch was in his bag and he had not wound it in months, since time did not matter very much during his journey west. He estimated they had been in the air for over thirty minutes when he first saw the green rising from the surrounding desert, lush in its color and dispersion.

Within the green rose the color of polished steel as the arcs and pillars of a city became visible. As the city grew closer the air car slightly dipped down to make its approach and land in a large, open area of concrete with sturdy buildings lining one side of it. They were buildings with large doors which Willem correctly guessed housed the air cars when not in use or for maintenance.

Standing in one area was a gathering of people in brightly colored clothing as if awaiting his arrival. The air car landed a moderate distance away from the crowd so as not to blow debris upon the bystanders then gracefully slid over near them presenting

Julia's side of the car to them. Willem looked around to see more men with weapons including some on top of the buildings watching the events unfurl.

Julia opened her door even before the fans cycled down and stepped out. Willem quickly moved with her and stepped as close to her as possible without touching her. She was still to his left giving him the ability to draw his revolver if necessary as they walked to the crowd of people. From the crowd three people stepped forward, two men and a woman all with greying hair and looking dignified in their pose. Julia directed him to the man in the middle of the three and stopped. She turned so she was between Willem and the elder gentleman of the group and introduced him to them.

"Willem, this is Jonah Treadwell, the head of our community."

The gentleman held his hand out to Willem. Willem took it and noticed how soft his hands were compared to the old man's hands at his approximate age.

"Mister Treadwell, it is a pleasure Sir."

"Willem, welcome to the community. Are you familiar with a Willem Forsyth?"

"No Sir, I have never heard that name before. Should I be?"

"There is some that think you might be a descendant of Mister Forsyth."

"Sorry, but I don't even know who my parents were. Is this important?"

"If you would be so generous as to let my medical staff test you, we might be able to determine your parentage. Also, you do not need your weapons here in the community."

"Mister Treadwell, my mind is the weapon. Whatever I put in my hands is nothing more than the tools to execute my thoughts."

Treadwell's eyes widened at the statement and his skin color slightly changed, paled at the thought of what the young man standing before him could possibly do.

"Yes, well, please surrender your tools then. As I said you will have no need for them."

Willem smiled as he unbuckled his gun belt and took it off. He refastened the belt then handed it to Julia without looking at her.

"Miss Malkin, do not lose this as it is my personal property whether you desire me to have them or not."

"I understand Willem." She spoke as she took the gun belt and carefully held on to it finding the weight was greater than she realized.

"Willem, we have quarters arranged for you, so you can get cleaned up and rest. It will take a bit to find clothing for you that will fit your large frame, but once your wagon arrives, your possessions will be brought to you in your quarters."

He indicated the woman standing beside him.

"Madeline will show you to your quarters and show you how to obtain a meal and such. Please, go with her and rest up, we can talk later once you are rested."

Willem followed the woman through the crowd as it parted for them. Past the buildings they got into a tubular vehicle that carried them into the community proper then transferred to another which took them to a building which she said was were his quarters would be located. She took him to the eighth floor and to a room that she said was to be his quarters during his stay in the community.

There was a sitting room with a medium size table for meals and such then another room which was the bedroom with a bathroom containing a shower. Willem was patient with Madeline as she showed him how to use the call buttons and the toilet facilities. He asked her if there was a place where he could have his hair cut and his beard shaved since any shaving items he owned were in his wagon. Madeline said she would send someone to take care of those things for him after he had time to shower then she left him alone.

Willem knew he was being watched and could only smile to himself that they would see nothing of value in his actions. He stripped in the bedroom and walked into the bathroom carrying his shoulder bag, laying in on the counter by the sink. As soon as he had the water temperature in the shower where he felt it was comfortable, he stepped in and just let the water flow over him. He always enjoyed the shower the old man had built, but it did not have the temperature control this one had. The only problem with this shower was that the shower head was not high enough for him to just stand up and let the water flow over his head.

The soap provided had a flowery fragrance to it, but it was what he had to use as he cleaned the ash from his face and beard. Once he finally felt he was as clean as he was going to get, he stepped out and a fan automatically came on above his head, blowing warm air down on him drying him off. Once dry he took the robe off the hook by the door and tried it on. It was too small for him even if the label in the robe said it was large.

The door signal sounded, and he just wrapped the robe around his waist as he moved to the door. A small screen by the door showed a young female standing outside waiting. He opened the door and smiled at the female who took a step back and looked up at him.

"May I help you?" He asked.

"Mister Willem, I am here to cut your hair and shave you. My name is Dorthea."

"Please come in. I apologize for my appearance, but this robe is too small to wear in a normal fashion, and my clothing is filthy."

"I understand Mister Willem."

Willem stepped back from the door and ushered her in. She looked around, then went to the table and set the small satchel she was carrying on it. She opened the satchel and laid out her instruments, then moved a chair out for Willem to sit on.

"Sir, would you please sit here so I can cut your hair."

Willem sat down making sure the robe covered him.

"Dorthea, please call me Willem. That is the only name I have, and it is not improper to address me in such a manner."

"Thank you, Willem. How would you like me to cut your hair?"

"Cut it however you think is best."

"Okay."

Dorthea went to work cutting his hair which was over shoulder length. She brushed it, then cut it, then brushed it again as she worked on his hair. Willem considered the woman working on his hair. She was moderately nice looking, standing maybe five feet five and smelled of roses. His mind wandered what a woman from this culture would be like to make love too, and Dorthea interested him.

Soon she had his hair cut and then asked him to lean his head back, so she could shave him. He asked for her to leave the mustache, but to neatly trim it. She had to straddle his leg at one point to insure she was giving him the best shave she could. When she finished, she straddled his leg again, wiped his face clean and moved his head side to side as she checked to make sure she had not missed any part of his face. Then she kissed him.

An hour later the door signal sounded again, and Willem left Dorthea asleep on his bed. A gentleman was standing in the hall waiting with what appeared to be so type of clothing in hand. Willem went back to the bedroom and closed the door before letting the man in.

The man had him try the overalls on and made notes concerning its fit and what adjustments would be needed to make it fit better. He told Willem this outfit would do until he could make him a proper set of clothing. The man never introduced himself and never mentioned Dorthea's instruments still laid out on the table.

Dorthea was up on her elbow as he walked back into the bedroom. She smiled at him and he just grinned as he removed the coveralls, then climbed back on the bed with her. Willem fell asleep afterwards and when he awoke she was gone, along with all her instruments. He smiled at the memory of the time with Dorthea knowing it would probably not repeat itself. But it also brought other things to mind, things he had to consider and maybe try again later.

Julia turned off the monitor in her office after viewing the events in Willem's bedroom. She knew Dorthea was not given to going to bed with just any man and her actions puzzled Julia. She had all but raped Willem as he sat in the chair, until he picked her up and carried her into the bedroom. Dorthea's actions were of deep desire and her vocalization during the act was loud. But then again Willem's manhood was larger than the average male within the community.

Willem ordered a meal which was brought to his door by a robotic cart. Willem gave the cart a quick examination before removing the plates and pitcher of tea to his table. The cart just remained in position as he ate then when after he put his empty dishes on the cart, it left without command. He had left his glass and half a pitcher of tea on the table, yet the cart left without them. That confirmed in Willem's mind that someone was watching him. The thought that they had watched him in the bedroom made him smile to himself.

Shortly after the cart had left, the man with his clothes returned with several outfits for Willem to try on to insure the adjustments were correct. The material was light and comfortable while the fit gave him plenty of movement. Once the gentleman left Willem gathered up his shoulder bag and decided it was time to examine the community he had entered.

When he stepped off the elevator, he was met by two of the Rangers who advised him they were to escort him where ever he went, and to insure he did not stray into a restricted area. Both men looked nervous with their assignment, so Willem decided not to push against their orders and just let them guide him. He told them to lead the way and show him the sights of the city, so he would not go someplace he was not allowed. This seemed to relax the men and he just smiled knowing that the places he did not go were places he wanted to go another time.

What no one considered was that Willem was wearing his calf high moccasins with his trouser legs pulled down over them. They took his firearms, but they had not even considered other weapons he might have with him. In the tops of each boot were thin knives, one on the inside and one on the outside of the boot top. Four knives total, each thin and razor sharp. Each was perfectly balanced for throwing and sturdy enough to use in a close combat fight. He had considered wearing the boots outside his trousers but knew that would draw attention to them and possibly the knives within.

Willem spent several hours just walking about the city seeing shops and where goods were sold and some of the manufacturing shops. He had been out for a couple of hours when one of his escorts advised him they were to take him to medical to check on his condition. They boarded a tube transport and within minutes arrived outside a building with a red cross on the front of it.

He was put through various tests and had his blood drawn. Willem never questioned what was happening as he knew if they had wanted to really cause him problems, they could have done that at any time he had stepped out of his room. When he was spoken to by the medical personal, they tried to explain what they were doing in the simplest terms they could use but Willem had read two different books written before the war and understood exactly what they were doing. He also knew his blood would be cross matched for DNA to determine his parentage if they had it on record.

Willem was taken back to his room after the examination. He ordered an evening meal and just waited, looking out his window at the crops growing in the distance until the sun went down and he decided to turn in for the evening.

He lay in his bed considering all he had seen today. Everything was clean and neat. Maybe to neat. His last thoughts before falling asleep was what was the purpose of the old man sending him here?

# The Box

Willem was taking breakfast when the door signaled a visitor. He instructed the door to allow entry and a dapper gentleman wearing a long, white coat who appeared in his forties entered the room.

"Willem, my name is Thomas Pollard and I manage the Metallurgical Lab. I have been instructed to take you to the lab and see what your box might contain."

"Do I have time to finish my meal?"

"Certainly Willem. Please, take your time."

Julia was once more watching Willem as he moved about his apartment and now as he ate his morning meal. She had the results of his DNA test on another monitor and there was no doubt about his parentage or ancestry. The council was meeting at that very moment to determine how to deal with Willem based on his DNA results.

It would be simple for Julia to enter the commands into her control panel to flood his rooms with a gas which would completely erase his memory, or even kill him, but as much as his presence scared her and the council, it had been forbidden.

Willem found his two escorts at the lower level once again as Pollard guided him to the tube transport car and they all traveled across the city to the Metallurgical Lab. His escorts never entered the lab and after a quick tour of the lab he handed his box over to Pollard.

Pollard first scanned the box for radioactivity as he explained every action to Willem. He stated that after the war, much of the metal found outside the community had retained levels of radioactivity from the bombs used to destroy the country. Pollard then explained that since they had no idea what was inside the box, they would use passive scanners to hopefully prevent the destruction of its contents.

During one scan they discovered micro-engraving on the end of the box. It was instructions on opening the box.

**"Stand box, this end up. Open with cold laser only."**

Pollard took the box to a machine, opened its cabinet door and set the box into a vise as instructed. Willem stood behind Pollard as he sat at the control desk and first aligned the laser to shave the end off the box. A quick diagnosis of the material gave Pollard the proper setting for cutting the end off. Pollard lowered the advised setting and made a trial cut to determine if alignment was correct then upped the power and sliced the end off the box.

After a few minutes to allow the gases to be cleared from the cabinet, Pollard opened the door and started to reach in to retrieve the box, but Willem took his arm and pulled him away from the cabinet opening.

Willem retrieved the box and took it to a nearby workbench and turned it upside down, dumping its contents on the bench. Several neatly folded pieces of paper fell out along with a crystalline cube approximately one inch on a side. Willem just looked at the items then spoke loudly.

"Julia, inform the council that I will meet with them and you as soon as my escorts can arrange transportation."

Julia sat in her office looking at her monitor as the shock of Willem calling out to her slowly passed. He knew he was being watched and who was watching him. This man scared her as she ordered transport for him to the council.

Willem carefully pushed the cube back into the box using the papers then put the papers back in the box without unfolding them to read what they contained. He thanked Pollard for his services and headed for the exit to the lab. His escorts were waiting for him with a small, four place air car. The trip across the city was quick and they landed on top of a building. His escorts took him down to the council room and stood outside as he entered.

The seven-person council was seated when he walked into the room along with Julia standing at one end of the council table waiting for him. He walked up to the table in front of Jonah Treadwell, the council chairman and dumped the box on the desk.

"So, Mister Treadwell, have the results of my DNA test came back yet?"

"You know about DNA testing?"

"I may have come from the outlands, but I am far from uneducated. By now you have had a chance to have the contents of my wagon examined, including the books I brought with me. If that was not a clue to what I am, then I suspect I'm talking to the wrong people."

"Willem, yes, we know your parentage. Who you are."

Treadwell ran his hand over his desktop controls and a hologram photo of a man and woman appeared above the desk.

"Do you know these people?"

"No, but then again the man is young, I only knew an old man. Are these my parents?"

"Yes."

Treadwell brought up a photo of the man, then morphed it to show a much older man.

"Mister Treadwell, this in inconclusive. I only have a memory of the old man with a full beard, and long grey hair."

Treadwell morphed the photo again adding a beard and greying the hair. Willem smiled at the hologram.

"Yes, that was the old man who raised me. He never told me he was my father, only that he was tasked to making a man out of me. What was his name?"

"His name was Winston Westbrook. Your mother's name was Cecilia Forsyth. She was the granddaughter of one of the three founding members of the community. This also makes you the only person alive that can trace their heritage to the founding."

Willem looked at the hologram of his parents. His father was as tall as he remembered before age took its toll on him. His mother was small, petite compared to him as she stood beside him. Willem looked down at the papers lying on the desk, picked the first one up and unfolded it. He took each folded paper and opened it and arranged them by importance.

There was a certificate of marriage between his parents. Then there was a certificate of his birth with his full name on it. Willem Walter Westbrook. Next was a certificate of his mother's death. It was dated three months after his birth. Cause of death was complications due to childbirth.

The last document in the group was the Last Will and Testament of Winston Westbrook. It had three witness signatures on it with their locations all being from the area Willem had been raised. The will gave Willem all that the old man owned, and all that his mother had inherited from her family, unless there were others alive to contest this portion of the will.

Willem handed the documents to Treadwell who read each one, then scanned them into the community's computer system. He sat for a minute looking at Willem who just stood waiting for the council to comment on his status. The computer gave a low ping and Treadwell looked down at his desk before speaking to Willem.

"Mister Willem Westbrook, the computer declares that the signature of Winston Westbrook is correct with the signature that is on file. Unless there is a challenge to these documents by a council member, I must declare them correct and advise you that you are now entitled to any, and all of the assets of the Forsyth and Westbrook family that has been held in trust within the community. This also gives you full citizenship within the community. Are there any protests to my decision?"

There were no comments from the council.

"Miss Malkin, please return all of Mister Westbrook's property to include firearms and escort him to the Forsyth estate so he can take possession of it. Mister Westbrook, there will be several documents for you to sign in order to take full possession of the estate and other properties within a few days. Do you have any questions of the council?"

"No Sir. I only request that any documents pertaining to the full assets of my inheritance be submitted to myself within the next two days, so I have a chance to see the extent of my properties."

"It will be so Mister Westbrook.   This meeting is adjourned."

Willem collected the documents, carefully folded them and placed them back in the box as he once more used them to push the cube back into the box.   Treadwell watched him and as Willem was picking up the box he spoke again.

"Mister Westbrook. Do you know what that cube is?"

"First of all, please call me Willem.   And no, not exactly. The old man told me many things about many wonders of life before and after the war.  Do you know what it is?"

"No, but there is reading on memory cubes that your father was working on before he left the community with your mother. But the writings are vague to say the least.  I noticed that you have not touched it with your fingers or flesh."

"The old man, my father, warned me there were many innocent things that should never be touched with the flesh unless a person is ready for the results, both good, or bad.  I'll deal with the cube in private."

"I understand Willem.  Please have a good day."

"And to you also Sir."

Willem never looked at Julia as he turned and walked from the council room. He walked directly to the lift that had brought him down from the roof and turned to see Julia walk in behind him along with his escorts. On the roof was now a larger air car waiting for him. He never spoke or gave any attention to Julia as he boarded the craft and took a seat. His escorts joined them after Julia was seated, facing towards him. Just as the craft was lifting off the roof Willem spoke to Julia.

"Did you enjoy watching me in my room with Dorthea?"

"What? What makes you think anyone has been watching you?"

"Julia, this will be the only warning I give you. Do not lie to me or be evasive in your answers to any of my questions. Where I come from the truth is honored above all else. Now answer my question."

"No Willem, I did not enjoy watching you with Dorthea. My assignment is the protection of the community and its citizens. You were an unknown at that time and precautions were taken to insure our safety."

"Are there surveillance systems at the estate you are taking me too?"

"Only on the outside to protect against intruders. The interior is void of sensors or micro-cameras."

"Thank you."

Neither spoke for the remainder of the trip to the estate. It was a sprawling, one level home with several outbuildings surrounded by trees and fields growing various crops. They landed in front of the main house and exited with the escort leading the way until they came to the porch where they took up positions on either side of the walkway facing away from the house. Julia walked to the front door and opened an access panel to the side of the door. She punched in a series of numbers and placed her eye to an optical scanner. First Willem heard the door locks disengage, then a rushing of air through small vents above the door.

"Willem, the house had been vacuumed sealed since the death of your grandfather, Godfrey Forsyth."

When the seals released the door, Julia opened it, then ushered Willem in following him into the house. They wandered through the house just looking in rooms as Julia had told him his Grandfather had died when she was a child and the house had been sealed ever since.

They located the kitchen to find it had been completely cleaned out of food stuffs prior to the house being sealed. She showed him how to us the kitchen's computer to order supplies for the kitchen. When he asked how those supplies would be paid she said the providers would submit their claim to the central system and his accounts would be debited and theirs credited once he showed receipt of the items.

There was a menu for selecting foodstuffs for delivery and Willem placed the order for a few items to give him a decent meal or two over the next couple days. He could fill his pantry later once he was settled in.

Julia told him his property would be brought to him that afternoon except for the horses and wagon as they were located at the community's stables and there was no place to keep the horses at the estate based upon the diagram she had on her wrist tablet. She also told him that any of the computers in the house could access the services available to him and all he had to do was to request a service and it would be provided in the same manner as his foodstuffs. She left him to discover the house that now belonged to him.

Willem found the study to be the place he would most likely spend the most time. It had two and a half walls covered with books and the wall to the outside of the house opened to a large, covered patio and garden. Even though the house had been sealed, the exterior grounds had been maintained along with flowers planted in the garden.

Papers were still laid on his grandfather's desk as if he had only left the study minutes before. As Willem looked through them he knew there was something he was missing. Something he

93

had been told or taught but could not put a finger on what it was he was missing. He thought it was not a safe place to keep important papers such as was on the desk then it dawned on him. Where did his grandfather keep important papers?

Willem looked at the computer on the desk and after a moment figured out how to power it up. He waited as it went through several operating tests then opened under voice command.

"Welcome back Doctor Forsyth."

Willem smiled and replied to the computer.

"Doctor Forsyth is deceased. I am Willem Westbrook, his grandson. Please explain how you work."

"All files are restricted. I have a Winston Westbrook on file, but your voice pattern does not match his. You are not allowed access to the files contained in my system."

"Computer, can you verify my right to access your files with the central computer due to the fact that both Doctor Forsyth and Winston Westbrook are deceased, and I am their heir to the estate?"

"One moment please."

Willem just leaned back in the chair as he waited for the computer to determine his status.

"Willem Westbrook. Would you submit to an optical scan, so I can link your voice to your identification?"

"Certainly. Where do I need to be?"

"Please face my monitor and do not move, I will take care of the scan."

Willem did as the computer asked and sat still as a red light flashed in his right eye. He had done an optical scan during his physical exams so understood his part in it. Once complete, the computer appeared to shut down and a moment then the screen changed to show what looked like a list of items stored on the computer.

"Willem Westbrook, this is your menu. You can access any file by verbal command or touching the file you wish to open."

"Thank you computer. Please put up a schematic of the floor plan of this estate."

Immediately a floor plan appeared, and Willem examined it. A small red dot showed in the study which Willem took to be him. To his left was a room marked as vault, but all Willem saw when he looked in that direction was a bookcase.

"Computer do you have the ability to open the vault?"

Immediately a portion of the bookcase swung open exposing the vault door then the vault door swung open. A moment after the door opened a light came on in the vault. Willem walked to the open vault door and looked inside. There were storage cabinets with drawers that were labeled plus tables with items on them. Willem walked back to the papers on the desk, gathered them up and placed them in the vault on a table for later examination.

"Computer, notate that the vault will be closed if I am not in this room, and will not be opened without my command."

"Willem Westbrook, I understand to seal the vault if you are not in the room, and only open the vault under your direct verbal command."

"Correct. If I were to say Jerome, open the vault. You will not open the vault until I say Peter, open the vault. This is a safety command in case I am in distress. Understood?"

"Question? Peter is to only be used to release the distress code?"

"Correct Computer. Are my commands understood?"

"They are understood and have been entered into my operating system."

"Computer do you also control the access to this house?"

"Yes, I can seal the house against intruders by your voice command to seal the house."

"Please seal the house now. I have a test to make and do now wish an intrusion."

"The house is sealed."

"Thank you."

Willem dumped the contents of the box on the desk. First, he took the papers and placed them in the vault then sat down and looked at the crystal cube sitting in front of him. He had a vague memory of his father telling him about a memory cube that if held it in the hand would transmit the information held within to the holder. But no one at the council table recognized the cube which made Willem wonder just where it came from.

"Computer, give me the history of Winston Westbrook."

Willem sat and watched photos move across the monitor as the computer gave the life on Winston Westbrook. It also covered the marriage of his father to his mother. Nothing within the computer told him why his parents had left the community. But his father was an engineer with studies in Chemistry. He was also the chief engineer for the community when he suddenly departed with his mother one night without giving a reason for his departure.

The program closed leaving Willem with more questions than answers. His parents were both classified as genius with his mother working in Psychology and Biology.

"Computer are you recording my presence within the study?"

"Yes, I record everything within the house except in the private quarters of the estate."

"Private quarters as in my bedroom?"

"Correct."

Willem carefully picked up the cube with paper left on the desk and went to the master bedroom. He sat in one of the arm chairs in the room and considered what he had to do next. Willem took a deep breath and dumped the cube into the palm of his left hand and closed his fist upon it. He could feel the cube heating up then his hand tingling before it seemed he was transported to another time and place.

Standing before him was his father without his beard and looking worn. He started talking by telling Willem his mother had just died from giving birth to him and that it was not his fault, but the fault of believing he could care for her during child birth. From there he explained why they had left the community as they both felt the direction it was taking was wrong. The man before him talked about the community then he talked about the love he had for Willem's mother and the son she gave birth too.

The old man went on to tell him how he intended to raise him if the spirits were willing and life in the hills cooperated. He then told Willem that during his growth he would teach him things he would know to unlock several secrets within the community. Secrets that agents within the community would find dangerous to their existence and be a danger to him. It would be up to him to sort out the information and to make the decisions he felt was best.

When the message was complete the crystal disintegrated in his fist. Willem opened his hand to see it had become nothing more that fine dust. He carefully stood and walked over to a trash container and poured the dust into it. Willem walked back to the study and instructed the computer to open the house.

Willem just moved around the house examining it and locating where things was situated. When the food stores were delivered he helped the deliveryman to stock the pantry and place those items needing refrigeration away. He signed for the food and thanked the man for delivering the items to him.

That afternoon his property was brought to him and he had it taken to one of the spare bedrooms. The food items he moved to the kitchen and put them away for later then went back for his clothing which he moved to his bedroom. His clothing from his temporary quarters were included and had been cleaned.

Willem knew there was much to do but today was not the day to do it. He looked through the books in the study and picked out one to read. It was 'The Tale of Two Cities' which he thought was a bit ironic given the situation he was now in.

He fixed a light evening meal and sat in the study reading until well past dark. Willem went to bed without thinking of a bed companion this night. He had other things on his mind and sex was not one of them.

# Empowerment

Willem took the strong box he had transported from Missouri into the study and placed it on a table in the vault and with a deft hand, unlocked it. He could tell there had been an attempt to open the box, but that attempt had failed. The gold and silver it contained was placed aside, but the notebook it contained was more valuable than all the gold and silver combined. It was his father's notebook and it was sealed by his father just before his death. Willem had promised the old man he would not open the notebook until he arrived at his destiny.

He broke the seal on the notebook and took a quick look through it. There were formulas and engineering diagrams contained with the notebook which Willem knew he would have to give serious study before he could determine what their purpose was or if they had any purpose at all.

Later in the morning, a gentleman arrived with an escort carrying a highly polished wooded case. From it he took the documents that finalized the transfer of Willem's inheritance to him. Willem read the ornate documents one at a time before signing them. As each was signed the gentleman placed a seal upon them verifying his signature as being true and valid.

The gentleman said the documents would be entered into the community's public records file, so everyone would know that the transfer of property and monies had taken place. He left a folder containing the complete inheritance for Willem to go over. With a stroke of the pen, Willem found he owned nearly a fourth of the community and more money than he felt he could ever spend.

He also had copies of the documents he had signed which told him of certain powers he now had within the community. One was that he could sit with the council and had a voice and vote at any meetings he decided to attend. Willem instructed the computer to keep him advised of all council meetings and the agendas for those meetings.

Willem still had a question in his mind he needed answering. When Linda had come to him in the barn it was after he had thought a lot about her beforehand. The same could be said about Gloria coming to his bed later. He wanted both females and they came to him without regard of the circumstances.

Later there was Darlene, the waitress in Green River. He wanted a woman, and she was unattached. The sex between them was unrestrained and very enjoyable, as she did everything possible to please him.

Then there was Dorthea. As she was cutting his hair he thought about how she smelled, all clean and the fragrance of her body as it was near his. When she first straddled his leg, so she could insure him a good shave, he thought about how nice it would be to feel her flesh against his. She was compliant to his desires in bed and never hesitated in her attempts to insure he was satisfied. Willem leaned back in the desk chair and focused on Dorthea and her body against his in the throes of passion. He visualized her naked body on his bed and her desire to make love to him. He held that thought for several minutes before relaxing his mind and moving on to other subjects while keeping that picture of her alive in his mind.

An hour later the computer announced a visitor at the front door. Willem looked at the monitor to see Dorthea standing at the door. He told the computer to allow her to enter and he met her in the large entry room of the house. She walked up to him and all but crawled up his tall body to kiss him. He carried her to bed and spent the rest of the day in bed with her as he exhausted himself with her.

Julia watched as Dorthea entered the house but had no visual contact on the interior. She knew that no communication had occurred between them but Dorthea had left her assigned workplace without comment and had gone to him. She pulled up the video of the two of them in the apartment and watched how Dorthea had acted with him and how he made love to Dorthea. Julia was still without a current lover and the look on Dorthea's face was one of fulfillment. This was something she longed for and was why she had gone through several lovers in search of such passion.

She shut down the video and went in search of a man, any man who would spend the night with her.

Willem let Dorthea sleep late the next morning as she had exhausted herself pleasing him. When she awoke, she spent the day with him moving around the house nude and ready for him when he desired her. She spent three days with him before he focused on her in his mind, giving her the freedom of her own desires and activities. Dorthea left after kissing him and telling him she enjoyed the time with him. He told her to advise anyone that would be upset with her absence to just tell them she was with him, and to file any complaint directly with him.

Somewhere in his father's notebook was the reason he could exert the power he had over the women who came to his bed. He thought back to the woman Margaret who had taken him into manhood. Had she stayed longer than she had bargained with his father because she wanted too, or because he wanted her too? Then there were the women he had taken in the villages. He tried to remember if he had silently desired them as he had Dorthea and they surrendered themselves to him, or was it something else? But one was a virgin who he took in one village. He suspected it was his silent desire that caused her to open herself to him.

This was something he needed to understand better, so he could control it better. This was not something he desired to be responsible for, but it was his to use and contain within his own mind. He also knew this was why he could sense fear in some people directed at him.

Willem spent the next week examining the files he found in the vault in a drawer marked as Doctor Cecilia Forsyth. As he read the files memories creeped into his mind of lessons long since learned yet forgotten. He remembered reading the Biology books from the fridge and asking many questions to gain a full understanding of the information.

One file opened a new line of questioning for him. It was a file on his mother's research in expanding the mind to utilize more of its capability. In it were chemical formulas for mind enhancement and notes attached to them regarding what level of success or failure of each formula on a test subject.

Willem compared the formulas to the formulas in his father's notebook and recognized this was his father's writing on the notes. He carefully went through the notebook until he came upon a formula conceived before his birth that was similar to the last one in the file. There was no notation concerning the application or testing of the formula, only that it had a 'star' in the upper corner of the page.

Moving further into his father's notebook he noticed that the scientific notations and research ended when he would have been about two years old. The notes after that were mostly metallurgical notes then he found a single note mixed in with other notes.

"W is exhibiting the effects Cecilia sought when she took the serum. His mind is open. I must be cautious when dealing with him to not allow him to influence my actions."

Willem closed his eyes and searched his memory, but nothing could be found to indicate what the old man was referring too. Then he had a sudden thought. If they were doing experiments in Missouri away from the community, where was the equipment, the lab for such work?

He went back to the computer and posted an inquiry concerning the disappearance of his parents. Willem asked if there was anything special missing from the community that might indicate they had taken the equipment with them necessary to continue the experiments they had been working on within the community.

It took the computer over an hour to produce a list of equipment and materials that the archives showed as missing in the days following his parent's disappearance. It showed a very large transport air truck was missing along with various laboratory equipment.

Willem had no memory of a vehicle or an elaborate lab, only the forge and the cabin. He had walked nearly every inch of the ridge and bottoms around the forge and never came upon anything that might even be considered unusual in nature. What had the old man done with the air truck and equipment?

What Willem was to never learn was that once his father had determined he had done all that could be done with the laboratory they had brought to Missouri, he had loaded everything back into the transporter insuring that he had what he needed for his forge then set the controls of the vehicle and sent it on its way. The transporter had all its vents open when it crashed into the Gulf of Mexico where it was resting on the sea floor.

Before he closed the house for the evening Willem had one last passing thought. Was he the result of a combination of his parents love for each other and a successful experiment?

# Rejection is also Success

After two weeks secluded in the house or the gardens behind the house, Willem decided he needed to go out into the community and see for himself why the people isolated themselves from the rest of the world. Especially since the technology within the community was centuries beyond what the rest of the world had at their fingertips.

Willem dressed as a local native in order not to cause any more problems than necessary other than his height giving away who he was. He was aware that the community knew of his existence but not who he actually was. He could sense the fear in people as he walked through the community and tried to emit a soothing feeling as he had no desire to harm anyone. Willem recognized he was a freak amongst these people with his tall stature and blond hair.

Julia had set the security sensors at the estate to advise her of any movement outside of the house and when he left, she was notified of his passage. He had summoned transport to retrieve him in front of the house and to deposit him in the middle of the business district of the community. She watched him through various sensors just walking around, looking into shops and just seeing what was available with his own eyes. He purchased a hat more suitable to the clothing he was wearing but otherwise was just sight-seeing.

Willem knew he was being watched and reached out to sense Julia watching him. The fact that he could do such things scared him because he knew it could be used for evil. It suddenly dawned on him that was most likely the reason his parents had fled the community. To prevent their research from falling into the hands of people who might use it for evil. He now knew where the undercurrent of fear was coming from. The people feared those in power.

In the market place, Willem placed an order for more foodstuffs for his pantry before returning to the estate. But before he entered the house he finally went to the out buildings to discover what they contained. One was a full laboratory capable of doing a variety of experiments. Another was a machine shop to construct about anything the mind could conceive. The third building was a storage building with boxes and crates neatly stacked. He knew he would soon have to explore this building to find what was hiding inside.

Back in the house he had the computer open the diagram of the estate and pin-pointed the location of stables he wanted built to have his horses nearby. The computer designed the stables and after two minor adjustments, he accepted the design and placed an order to have it built within the week. The computer advised him the order had gone out and had been accepted and that construction would begin the next day.

Julia had used four lovers since Willem's arrival and she could not find the satisfaction that she desired. She flew her personal air car to the estate and landed in front of the house. As she approached the front door it opened for her to enter. She could see Willem standing across the main room waiting for her. As the door closed behind her she opened the top of her coveralls and pulled it down exposing her large breasts, unencumbered by a bra. She was walking towards him as she did this and was unfastening the belt around her waist to further remove her coveralls when Willem acted.

He focused on her, stopping her in mid-stride freezing her in place. He walked up to her and moved around her as her eyes were focused on where he had been standing, not where he was currently at. He walked around her, studying her as he probed her mind. He sensed her sexual desires for him but overlaying that was the desire for power. Power to control all she envisioned. He was right the night they met that she might be sexually desirable, but she was not someone he wanted in his bed.

Willem continued his experiment with her as he reached out and grasped one of her large, firm breasts and squeezed it hard. No reaction to his touch appeared on her face or in her mind. He cruelly twisted her breast and still no reaction, pain or pleasure. He released her breast, stepped back, and told her to cover herself which she did without any emotion.

His final mental command was for her to return to her office without memory of coming to his home. She turned and went back out the door and to her air car. He kept his mind linked to hers, listening for anything that might show she was only playing at following his commands. Willem could see through her eyes as she landed, then went to her office. He maintained the link to her as he completely released her. At that moment she nearly doubled over and cried out from the pain in her left breast from his cruel treatment of it. She could not understand why she was experiencing the pain and went into her private toilet facilities, lowered her top to see the bruising of her breast linking the pain she was feeling to the bruising.

Willem watched through her eyes as she checked her log to see she had left her office for nearly an hour. Checking her air cars routing data, she learned she had gone out to the estate, and video of the outside grounds showed she had entered, then left a short time later to return to her office. She had no memory of any of this and she became frightened at what had happened to her. Willem broke the link with her mind, and he felt the fear of having more power than any single individual should possess.

Dorthea came to visit him late in the afternoon without being summoned. She told him she had a couple of days off and could think of no better way to spend them unless he had other plans, or other ladies to take care of. He only contacted her mind to insure she was there of her own free will and not coerced by another to possibly spy on him. Willem found her to be eager to please and be pleased in their couplings. The only mental contact he had with her during the time she spent with her was to find out what she desired and did all he could to fulfill his end of the relationship.

It was also during this time he remembered he should have children by Gloria and Linda by this time. This was a responsibility he knew he had to deal with as soon as possible. He was not concerned with Dorthea becoming pregnant as he knew she was taking precautions, a manner of birth control now being used within the community, but Gloria and Linda had no options when they gave themselves to him.

After Dorthea left, Willem began planning a trip back to Kansas to deal with the possibility of his children.

# Bird's Eye View of Kansas

Willem determined that using a long-range drone to do the basic check on the children was the simplest method until he could arrange to go back to Kansas and hopefully insure his children were being taken care of. Even though he was raised by his father, Willem always considered himself an orphan.

In requesting the drone mission, he had to have direct contact with Julia. He kept the contact polite and informal as possible while feeling near fright from her to have him in the same room with her. He made no intrusion into her mind to gain advantage over her, but laid out his reason for the use of a long-range drone out as clearly as possible.

If he had children by the two females, then they were by birthright members of the community and should be brought into the community to insure their growth and protection. Willem had done his research and quoted several points of order in the community's charter concerning the care and welfare of membership children. All that would be required was a positive DNA test of the children to prove if they existed, they were from him and not another man.

The first step was the discovery of the fact he had children by these two females. Once it was shown the children did exist, then an attempt would be made to prove they were his children and bring them into the community to live on Willem's estate.

Julia had no choice but to approve Willem's request and notified the council of the action. One protest was made against the action, but was quelled by the articles of charter in Willem's favor. The drone was launched within an hour of Julia's notification to the council and Willem was in the drone controllers room watching as it flew east towards Kansas.

Finding the farm was easier than Willem suspected, but the discovery of any children would take time. It was spring in Kansas and the drone flew a high-altitude race track pattern above the farm house watching for any sign of infants with parents. Late on the third morning after arrival, Willem was able to identify Linda as she took clothes out to hang up to dry. She had a toddler with her that after she had hung up the clothes, breast fed the child before going back into the house. It was then Willem remembered he had turned twenty-three only weeks before without ceremony. But the one child was proof enough for Willem to put the next part of his plan in operation. Especially since the child appeared to have blond hair.

Willem's plan was to take him along with the horse and wagon back to Kansas in an enclosed transporter to an area within ten miles of the farm. The drone showed the area to be isolated and there was nothing there to hinder their arrival during the night.

During Willem's research, he found that the medical department had a small, hand-held DNA tester that he could carry in his shoulder bag and test the children to insure they were his.

114

The Council ordered four men from the security detachment to accompany him as far as the landing site, and stay there to insure they were not discovered. Willem would also have a small communicator, so he could communicate with the truck and guards. They would also take two one-person skimmers in case Willem found himself in a situation needing help.

Willem was told he would have to foot the expense of this enterprise, and he told Julia that when he returned, he would gladly sign off on the transfer of funds to pay the expenses for the trip.

When Willem met the men that would be going with him, he entered their minds to find out what their instructions were for this enterprise. He found that one had been a lover of Julia on several occasions, and had spent the previous evening with her. He had orders to kill Willem if the opportunity presented itself in a manner that would not be suspicious. Willem altered the man's thinking developing intense loyalty towards Willem.

Willem knew that once he returned from Kansas, he would have to deal with Julia, but how was still a vacant idea in his own mind.

The trip to Kansas went without incident as the drone guided them past the small populated areas enroute. They landed three hours before dawn to give Willem the time for his horse to recover from the sedation it was given so they could transport it. It was still dark when Willem headed for the farm to see if the child, or children were in fact his. In his shoulder bag were twelve gold coins he was prepared to give Susan's brother-in-law if need be to secure their freedom from working on the farm.

Willem arrived at the farm just after nine in the morning. He was dressed in his buckskins with his gun belt on and ready for any trouble that might arise. Willem was barely off the wagon when Gloria stepped out of the house with a child in her arms. She smiled at Willem and turned back to the house and called for Linda to join her because Willem was here. It only took a minute before Linda came out with a blond-haired child in her arms.

Both women came off the porch and met Willem as he walked to them. He hugged and kissed both women, then looked at the children they were holding. Gloria spoke first.

"Willem, this is your son William."

Willem took the dark-haired boy from her and held him up to look at him. The boy's blue eyes sparkled, and Willem could feel happiness from the child as he was being held. Linda then introduced him to his daughter Martha. He handed William back to Gloria and took Martha from Linda. She also had blue eyes, but was not as happy as William was to be held by a stranger. Willem gently slipped into her young mind and gave her a sense of happiness and love. He kissed her on the cheek before handing her back to Linda.

"I've came to take you back with me. I have a place far to the west for all of us."

"Does that include Mike?" Susan asked.

"Yes Gloria, he is your son."

"He's in the fields with his Uncle Henry. When do we have to leave?"

"No later than tomorrow morning, and all you will need is what will fit in my wagon. Leave everything else."

As the women were packing, Willem was watching the children. During this time, he tested each child for DNA without harming either child. His DNA was already entered into the device and both times it showed the children were his. The device was linked to his small communicator which was linked to the drone high above them. The information was transmitted back to the community to become part of the public record.

Willem thought about another young girl named Martha that had been raped on the road to Coffeyville. He swore to himself that his Martha would never be put into such a situation. She would be protected, even if he had to sacrifice himself to insure her safety.

Mike and his Uncle Henry returned from the fields before noon and after some discussion, Mike asked to stay with Uncle Henry. Willem had no influence in his decision and stayed out of

117

the discussion between Mike and Gloria. Gloria relented knowing that they would be leaving Henry alone to work the farm.

They stayed the night at the farm with Willem sleeping under his wagon away from both women. He knew he would sleep with them again, but after they had been given birth control to prevent any more pregnancies.

Before they left in the morning, Willem gave Henry the small pouch containing the gold coins. Gloria cried a bit knowing she was leaving Mike behind, but Willem told her if things worked out, she could return to visit in a few years. He had called ahead to let the security team know he was enroute, and as they traveled, he slipped into both women's minds to ease the way for them to experience something they had never dreamed of.

Willem had arranged the wagon so there was a large place in the middle that was padded with quilts and bear skin for the babies to play in during the flight. Neither female acted as if this was strange to them as they also rode in the wagon which had been tied down inside the van portion of the air truck.

The truck landed on top of the medical facility and Willem told the women to go with the people who would insure they were in good health, and would also check on the babies to insure they also were in good condition. He did a quick scan of the medical personal to see if there was any malice towards the females or children.  Willem found none, but planted the idea of great harm to the person who harmed one of his children, or their mothers.

Willem went back to the estate with the horse and wagon and just waited until the medical personal were finished with his new family.  He had left the one guard that he had adjusted his attitude towards Willem behind with another guard to insure his family was safely brought to the estate once released.

As he sat in his study watching a link to the medical center's security system as his children were being poked and prodded to insure their health, Willem considered his position in all of this once again.  His unwanted ability had created the situation of having two children to be concerned with now placed him in the position of being responsible for their lives from now until they reached maturity.  Willem had no feelings other than responsibility for either mother, and knew that unless he went into their minds, they would expect him to sleep with them from time to time.

Gloria was ten years older than Willem having Linda at the age of fourteen.  The estate had plenty of room for this new family and then some.  Once the children grew older they would have their own rooms in the estate, but until then, he had cribs brought in and placed in the rooms that their mothers would occupy.  He had also arranged for the women to receive an education while with him to move about in this world.

The family arrived at the estate just before dark. He showed the women to their rooms and explained to both he would come to them, but they were not to come to him in his bedroom unless they were invited by him. They understood, and Gloria even mentioned that he had other lovers to consider. Willem told them he did have another lover, but he was only trying to be fair to the both of them. They had eaten at the medical center and turned in after seeing to the babies and their needs. Willem slept alone pondering his next step. The one in dealing with Julia.

# Dealing with a Witch

The next night after returning from Kansas, Willem sat in his darkened study and slowly sought out, then entered Julia's mind. She was very upset that Willem had returned and was plotting a way to get back at her former lover who was to kill him, but instead became a loyal guard now under Willem's employment along with the other three than had gone to Kansas. Willem was going to recruit his own security force as granted by the community's charter to the founders.

For the first time, Willem went deep into a person's mind searching for any thread to use against them. Even as soft as his touch was, he soon felt the headache his subject was experiencing by his presence in their mind. He smiled at the thought of discomfort he was causing Julia as he searched her mind. Finally, he found something that played in his favor. She had corrupted three of the council members, placing them in a position to support her slow movement to more power, and then control of the community.

Willem was still haunted by the deaths of the men he had killed during his journey to Utah, even if those men deserved to die. But Julia was frightened by Willem even before she knew who he was, and now wanted him and his off-spring dead because of their ties to the Forsyth/Westbrook legacy within the community. He came here with no malice towards anyone, but now with his children in danger, he felt, for the first time, malice towards another.

He left her mind leaving her with a severe headache and balled up in the fetal position on her bed from stomach cramps. Willem left the study and looked in on the children. The house was quiet, and he went to bed with the feeling great things were possible if he could only stay alive to help them along.

For the next week he kept Julia in a constant state of pain and confusion as his own mind opened even more to the possibilities of the power his parents had given him. He made love to Gloria one night, then Linda the next, as they tended to the house and gardens. Both learned how to use the kitchen and its foreign instruments for preparing meals. His funds were nearly unlimited as he recruited a dozen more men to act as his personal security with their primary function to protect his children and their mothers.

When Julia learned of his private security team, she became violent in the privacy of her office. Willem just observed the incident, then sent her into another series of painful cramps that forced her into the medical center for treatment.

Willem came to realize he was torturing Julia, using her thoughts of removing not only himself, but his children from the living as an excuse to abuse her. He suddenly recognized that made him no better than her and released her from her pain.

Willem's father had taught him to never abuse an animal, and there was no doubt Julia was an animal that walked on two legs.

He had a thought and opened the computer to do a search for him. Was there any link between Julia Malkin and either the Forsyth or Westbrook family's? The answer came back almost immediately. Julia was a distant cousin on his Forsyth grandmother's side. This cleared up a small detail that he had not pursued when he was told he was the only individual alive with a direct connection to Doctor Forsyth. Willem found that Julia had twice petitioned the council to gain access to the Forsyth estate and had been denied because there was no evidence of the death of Cecilia Forsyth/Westbrook. Without that proof, and proof of no children by Cecilia Forsyth/Westbrook, there could be no release of the trust for another eleven years.

Once more he softly entered her mind and moved through it as she slept looking for her reasons for her actions. He found her desires for sexual contact to be two-fold. She wanted him in a purely sexual way, but she hoped to become pregnant by him to close the connection to the estate. Once a child was conceived, she planned to remove Willem from the picture and take over the estate, giving her nearly unlimited power over the council. When that failed, she wanted him eliminated so she could cancel out the waiting period and take control. His children only made this more difficult, but she was plotting to remove them also in various ways over the years.

Julia Malkin was power hungry and had used her body to gain much of what she had in life. Her mind was open to him and he learned she was responsible for the deaths of two individuals who she felt was a hindrance to her move to power. Julia had also undermined the actions of one councilman in opening the council to those she considered inferior. She also was blackmailing three of the current council members who she had either perverted with her body, or she had discovered things in their private lives that would have them removed from the council.

Willem could not find the source of her greed for power, or what brought about the hatred for how things were being done. He only found the thought that she was superior to those exercising power within the community. Willem spent the rest of the night examining the protocols in place within the community that were designed to prevent such people, megalomaniacs, from gaining power and establishing what would be a dictatorship over the community. Somehow Julia had managed to either fool those tests, or sidestepped them in her climb to power.

Somewhere in the files in the vault, Willem felt there was an answer to this problem of how Julia had managed to avoid detection all these years. Julia was three years older than Willem, and she had commented she was a small child when Doctor Forsyth had died. Could Julia be the result of a similar experiment that created him without the physic abilities he now processed? Such a search of the vast number of files in the vault could take weeks or even months to discover, and during that time Julia would be free to further develop her own plans to remove his family.

Willem walked out into the gardens into the darkness of pre-dawn and stood thinking about his father and all he had been taught. The research his parents had done, had completed, was a danger to mankind if it had fell into the wrong hands. Willem speculated this was why they had left the community. He decided they had left so they could continue the research without interference or fear of it becoming a weapon to use against the rest of the world. His father had raised him to respect others regardless of conditions, and even having to kill those that meant harm to others or himself was only a human condition that had to be dealt with.

It was time to end this with Julia. She had no feelings towards humanity, only her own selfish greed for power. Only he knew of her responsibility in the deaths of two people who she felt stood in her way to power. Willem knew he could not take this to the council without exposing himself and his abilities to the world. This would create a climate of fear against himself, then his children that would be an even greater danger. It was time to end this once and for all.

Willem stood in the garden smelling the faint odor of the flowers as he went further into his own mind, and then the mind of Julia Malkin as she slept in her medical bed at the medical center.

Julia became awake in her own mind and could see Willem standing at the foot of her bed wearing his buckskins and his pistol belt. She threw off her covers to expose her nude body to him and raised her arms as she spread her legs wanting him to come to her. But this was not his purpose as he calmly drew his handgun from his right holster and shot her in the head.

The medical bed registered Julia's heart stopping, and all signs of life fade away as it alerted the medical staff of her condition. They found her uncovered with her legs spread and knees in the air as if taking a lover, but there were no marks to be found on her body. With Julia dead, there was no longer a link to her or her room for Willem to observe the events of her discovery.

Willem stood in the cool of the morning air and shivered at what he had done. He felt remorse at killing Julia because she was still a human being. Willem knew that he could have loved her, and made love to her if her heart was not black with the desire for power beyond her fingertips.

He stood and considered his own situation. No single person should have the power he just demonstrated against Julia. Willem felt he should end his own life to protect those against him from his ability to harm them in such a personal way. But inside his home were two children carrying his DNA. Could they have inherited his abilities considering he was the result of his mother taking a serum that produced his abilities? He had to stay alive to prevent one of his children from becoming a Julia with powers no man should possess.

Willem went to bed with the feeling of a piece of him detached from him for killing Julia.

A scan of Julia's brain showed a massive cerebral hemorrhage which caused her death and no reason could be determined for such an incident. Willem later read the report knowing that it was caused by a bullet entering her brain. A bullet that only existed in her mind at the time of her death.

As the news of Julia's death became public, Willem could sense relief spread across the city. The dread he once felt slowly gave way to promise of a bright future. The man who replaced Julia brought a sense of compassion to the Security office.

# Moving Onward

One of Willem's greatest fears was that he would become overwhelmed by the thoughts and emotions of the people around him as his own mind became more open and receptive. He found he could turn off that part of his senses, as if throwing a switch which allowed him to interact with people, but he never lost the basic feelings some people had towards him, or others around him.

Willem took interest in the activities of the city, often attending the Council meetings, but only spoke when a question was directed at him. He did submit a proposal to the Council to increase the funding for the Community Theater Group. Willem offered to meet, dollar for dollar, the increases the Council made to the Group without conditions.

He also learned as time progressed, so did his ability to absorb and retain information as his own knowledge of mathematics, chemistry, biology and other sciences were made known to him as he read every book he could lay his hands on. His memory of what he read was always concise to include the page number of what book he had read it in. It would take Willem a decade to go through the boxes in the storage building, reading every book or file found in the boxes. He discovered old technology that with minor improvements, made the lives of the people easier in many areas.

Willem moved through life managing his estate and watching his children grow. William showed no signs of having any of the abilities of his father, but Martha did appear to have a piece of his abilities. Willem went into Martha's mind and closed that portion off from her consciousness in hopes that she would never be able to unlock them until he could teach her as his father had taught him. Both were highly intelligent and took to their lessons early in their lives.

Gloria and Linda were educated with his help, opening their minds to new ideas and concepts. By the time the kids were five years of age, both had completed high school and were working on college level courses and could handle any conversation with members of the community without fear of being ashamed of their upbringing.

Both females also understood Willem's position within the family. He never felt love for them as he might if he was normal, but he cared for them as if they were his wives in the fullest sense. His love making with either female was honest, and they never asked for any more than what he could give them.

The children were in their seventh year when Willem met a young woman that took his heart. Her name was Marissa and he never made any attempt to mentally seduce her as he had others over the years. He was now thirty and she was barely twenty when he met her in the market. Willem would stop by her stall every day to talk to her and finally asked her to his estate for dinner.

Marissa knew he had two women living with him, and he explained the situation as best he could. She already knew they were outlanders and mothers of his children. But there was no official record of marriage between him and them. He talked to Gloria and Linda about Marissa and both understood his feelings towards them. Willem never denied he had strong feelings for the mothers of his children, but never truly loved them.

Both women knew they were not exclusive to him, and they had even gone out and taken other lovers outside the estate over the years. Willem had lovers at the estate which at first seemed awkward until the women told him they understood and would never hinder any relationship he developed. All the three of them were concerned about was the children. Any sexual activity between them was just human nature.

Willem dated Marissa for three months, having her to the estate for dinner, or taking her to concerts and plays during this time. He never touched her in any manner that was suggestive and certainly blocked his mind from hers to prevent any false feelings between them. It was Marissa's idea to spend their first night together in her own apartment.

For six months, any night they spent together was in her apartment as she did not wish to be a problem with the women living with him. It was Linda who finally broached the subject of Marissa sleeping with Willem when she was over for dinner one evening. Linda told her they understood Willem's feelings and respected them.  Marissa asked if either of the women were sleeping with Willem and Gloria told her that they had often slept with Willem, but had not spent a single night with him since he started dating her.

Willem married Marissa a year after meeting her, and they spent a month in a cabin he had built away from the community in the Rockies.  The children took to Marissa and life was pleasant for Willem as the women became good friends, often shopping together and having parties during the day with other women they had met.  Gloria and Linda dated more now and had a string of lovers to provide them with the pleasure that Willem reserved for his wife.

Marissa became pregnant two years after their wedding. She told Willem he could sleep with Gloria and Linda during this time if he felt the desire, but he never left their bed for another. Willem entered Marissa's mind only once before he asked her to marry him to determine her true feelings for him.  He knew it was a risk, but he found her love for him to be genuine.

Willem became the father of another son who he named Winston after his own father.  He never interfered in his father-in-law's business within the market, but insured when times were slow his father did not have to worry about his business.  Willem even supported his move into other markets.

Marissa became pregnant again when Winston was four and gave him another son which she named Craig after her own father. All of Willem's children bonded with the elder children often taking care of their younger siblings and even helping them with their studies. Neither of the children by Marissa exhibited any special talents other than the ability to learn at an early age.

Willem had spent months going through his grandfather's files examining them for anything that he could use to further progress humanity. He also compared them to his father's notebook. Buried in his father's notebook were three segments of a chemical formula that taken by themselves were useless but when combined gave him the formula of the serum his mother had taken. He built files of all his father's work but left out the completed formula before having the notebook sealed in a display with it opened to a simple formula for composite steel that he introduced to the community.

As the children aged, he took them back to the Missouri hills to see how he was raised and lived in the cabins as he once lived. He had rebuilt the cabins as they once were without all the amenities the children had grown up with and they learned how to survive as he did without much of the comforts of the community. They learned of hunger and how to find food in nature.

One thing that Willem did was to search the hills surrounding the cabin for the grave of his mother. Even with the technology available to him, it took almost two months to locate her grave, far into the hills where it was marked with a single slab of stone with the words 'Beloved" cut into it.  Once the remains were uncovered and DNA tested, her remains were moved to lay next to his father's and proper headstones placed on both graves.

He never learned why his father had isolated his mother's grave from their homestead, but remembered how the old man had often left by himself in the direction of the grave, to return hours later looking sad.

Willem taught his sons how to work raw steel into tools and back at the community, he had a blacksmith shop built so he could continue their education as they studied engineering and chemistry.  Martha turned her studies towards Botany after her first trip into the hills of Missouri to help find food sources not only for herself and siblings, but to enhance the lives of the people who were still living life, decades away from the life she lived in the community.

Gloria returned to Kansas several times over the years to visit with Mike as he grew into a good man and married.  She became the grandmother to five children by Mike and his wife as he not only farmed but ranched, raising cattle for the growing market.

She met a lab technician from the Metallurgical lab who had come to the estate to discuss an adaption of the steel formula with Willem.  A year later they married with the blessing of

Willem and the children. Gloria gave him twins two years later. William stayed in his father's house giving his mother the chance to have her own life.

Linda married a lieutenant in Willem's private security force and gave him three children until they determined the family was large enough.

Willem insured both women were taken care of and their children had the best education the community could provide.

Slowly, with the help of his children, Willem would open the community to the outside world. He knew it was a risk, but he also hoped he had designed the safeguards well enough to prevent any major problems.

There was one attempt by the government of the reconstructed United States to take control of the knowledge and resources of the community, but Willem stopped it cold. It was not with the power of his mind, but with the knowledge of how to destroy all that had been rebuilt over the decades. Willem was sixty-three when this happened, as he stood on the road leading into the community dressed in his buckskins, and defied the leaders trying to force their way into the community to take control of it.

The vehicles the government were using were primitive and he shut them down with the technology he had at hand. An air car flew along the left flank of the convoy of trucks and troops dropping smoke bombs over two hundred meters from the convoy. Willem told the leaders the next air car would drop explosives along the convoy destroying it and killing as many men as possible, plus just out of sight was hidden an army with far superior weapons to deal with any survivors.

One leader asked what would happen if they just killed him and proceeded on to the community. Willem only smiled and said then all lives would be forfeit and once again the community would close itself off from humanity.

Ultimately ambassadors would be exchanged between the community and the government. Craig Westbrook went to capital in Ohio as the first ambassador to the government.

Willem lived a quiet life as he attended to the research his father and grandfather started decades before his birth. His estate grew with new discoveries from his lab with the help of his children and grandchildren.

The old cabin in Missouri was visited as often as possible by Willem and his descendants. He had posted a security detachment there to protect the cabin and forge from those who might destroy it. Several of the men he posted there took local wives as a community grew around the forge. As modern as the guards' quarters were, the cabins were never modernized. As with his children, his grandchildren learned to survive in such an environment with William's son, Robert moving into the cabin to live for over a decade as his grandfather once had. Robert grew to be a tall, strong man like Willem with blond hair and blue eyes.

The community sent out doctors and technicians out into the growing world and took some outlanders in to train them.

Willem had opened the community up to the world and in doing so grew the importance of education. What he had discovered in his research of his grandfather's files was this was the original intent of the community. To survive the holocaust the world had experienced, then to help rebuild it. This concept was lost once Willem's great-grandfather had died and his own grandfather kept that a secret as he worked to find ways to strengthen the community while preparing to open it to the public. He died before he felt the community was ready to open its door to the world.

# Time stops for no man

After sixty-one years of marriage, Marissa died in Willem's arms as he finally told her about his unique abilities. He entered her mind, so she could feel the pain of his love for her as she was dying, and she returned her love the best she could in her condition. They were linked in such a manner when she took her last breath.

Willem turned his mind inward and ended his own life as he held Marissa in his arms. He had done all he could and at the age of ninety-two, he was tired even if he still had a decade or more of life in his body. His last act was to send out his love to his children and their children, and the challenge to continue his work to improve mankind.

Martha had unlocked her barriers to her own abilities decades earlier and had learned the danger of having them. She never used them as she grew older knowing the pain it had caused her father over the years. She watched her own children along with the nieces and nephews of the family for these abilities. Martha would watch four generations for these talents before she concluded they had ended with her.

The Westbrook family expanded sending family members out into the world to continue the work of Willem Westbrook. They went overseas to help find a way for the world to unit. Two were killed during these attempts, but that never stopped them from trying.

The only monument to Willem Westbrook was the crypt, he and Marissa were buried in. Every attempt by the community to erect a monument to Willem was shot down by the family. As wealthy and powerful the family had become over the decades they never forgot the people that needed help regardless of their circumstances.

But his Grandson Robert did build not one, but over a dozen monuments to Willem. Robert built library's all over the country and filled it with books printed in a publishing house he built. Books of all type were copied and printed regardless of their age or subject matter. If a book turned up that had not been printed at the time of discovery, it was immediately taken to the presses.

No matter the location, the library that was built had engraved in the stone above the door; The Willem Westbrook Library.

# Willem's Legacy

This was the legacy of Willem Westbrook. A passage from an old book which had long been removed from the people, yet he had a copy that he had been raised with. That book rested in a sealed case positioned in the main room of the house on the estate open to a page with that passage marked.

"Do Unto Others, As You Would Have Them Do Unto You."

# About The Author

Leon Michaels is the author of several novels and short stories that reflect his twenty-three years of military service.  Michaels enlisted in the Marine Corps in 1970 and has memberships in the Veterans of Foreign Wars, the American Legion, the Disabled American Veterans organizations, NRA, and Rotary International.  In 1971, he married his high school sweetheart, raised three daughters and has three grandsons. He calls Creek County, Oklahoma home.

Made in the USA
Columbia, SC
09 July 2018